"Whoever loves on Pawnee Rock will love always and always," she murmured softly.

The Corner Stone

(Annotated)

by

Margaret Hill McCarter

Author of
"The Peace of the Solomon Valley,"
"The Price of the Prairie," Etc.,

Illustrated by
J. Allen St. John

Chicago
A. C. McClurg & Co.
1915

Annotated by
Barbara A. B. Seiders

West Richland, Washington
One Hundred Year Horizons
2012

THIS LITTLE STORY is offered to such as hold it good to believe that, in this practical old world, the things that are not seen are greater than the things that are seen; and that sometimes the eyes of innocence and love and trust—even the eyes of a little child—can look far into the real heart of life.

Skies of Pearl O'er Prairies Green

The Corner Stone

I

We may build more splendid habitations,
Fill our rooms with paintings and with sculpture,
     But we cannot
Buy with gold the old associations.
                              — Longfellow.

MAY air, shot through with gladsome morning light, overhung all the prairies, swathing the brow of old Pawnee Rock with a diaphanous veil filmy and fine as the draperies the master painters once drew about the shoulders of rare old Madonnas. Wide away the landscape stretches in lengths of shimmering green checked across by flat brown roadways, and melting at last into a mist of lavender-gray. The only break in all this level realm is Pawnee Rock — grand old citadel of the Plains, upreared in its majestic loneliness — the watch tower of the prairies through uncounted centuries.

The westbound Santa Fe train was swinging away down its shining trail of steel, its coil of silvery smoke untwisting behind it. In the observation car Edith Grannell watched the land waves roll by with face aglow. Hers was an attractive face, with sunny, gray eyes shaded by dark lashes, straight black brows, a mouth and chin bespeaking character, with a sense of humor in the little upcurve of the lips; while from the pile of lustrous brown hair to the firm white throat between the lines of the soft linen collar there was the mark of dainty, cleanly, healthy youth. A keen reader of human nature might sometimes catch the sweep of a quickly vanishing shadow coming into the gray eyes now and then, token of a deeper feeling than most light-hearted girls of twenty-two possess.

It came into her eyes this morning as she took in the passing view. It was not her first sight of the prairies. The happiest part of her orphaned childhood had been spent on her uncle's ranch in the West, and now he had written to her to come again for a summer's visit to this place of cherished memory.

"I wonder if Uncle Samson will know me. It has been twelve years since I was here." The gray eyes darkened momentarily.

"Twelve years in boarding schools, with chaperons in vacations! I've never seen Uncle Samson once in all this time, and he's the only other Grannell in the world, so far as I know. I wonder why he never asked me to visit him before. Or rather why he should write me now to spend the summer here."

The shadow vanished from her eyes as she added: "He's been good to me in his way; I'm not going to find fault. And now that I can take care of myself, I hope I can make some returns for the money he has spent on my education, and" — there was a little choking pain in her throat — "it will be good to feel that there is some place that seems something like a home. I've been homeless so long."

On this May morning, Samson Grannell, rich ranch owner in the great Kansas wheat belt, was motoring up to the village to meet the train. He did not notice anything of rock, or sky, or fleeting purple cloud-shadows on green prairies. What he did note was the thrifty promise of June in the wheat fields and the straight lines of the long narrow roadways between them. His mind this morning, however, was not altogether with his eyes on the wheat fields and roadways. While they lost nothing of the commercial value of the landscape, he was busy with plans of his own.

"Edith is under obligation to me before everybody else," he mused. "I've supported her and educated her, and I'm the only living person to be interested in her welfare. Now if she is a sensible girl, this will be the biggest thing of all if my plans carry — and they will carry."

As he sent his big car swiftly along the level road against which the seas of green wheat were surging like ocean tides about a bar of level sand, Grannell did not repeat even to himself what this biggest thing of all might be. But the square-cut jaw was index to how well any plan of his must thrive when he said, "It will carry."

At the station he did not go forward to meet his niece climbing down from the Pullman beyond the water tank. Everything, including nieces, came to him.

"You are Edith, I suppose." He gave her his hand as if to ward off a more affectionate greeting, just as twelve years ago at this very place he had given her his hand to ward off a more affectionate parting. But the young lady who met him showed no signs of tumultuous effusion. Instead of the shy little child whom he was unconsciously expecting, came a girl with shining eyes and lustrous hair and cheeks of apple blossom pink; a girl with the vigor and health and grace of youth.

The gown of dark-blue soft stuff, finished with the embroidered linen collar and cuffs, the stylish little blue straw hat with white quill things of latest millinery fashion, the dainty white-stitched blue gloves — even the quaint little monogram pin,

wrought in gold, the finishing ornament below the V-shaped collar opening that left the white throat free — not a feature was as Grannell had unconsciously pictured. And least of all had he anticipated the certain, indefinable air of self-control and self-reliance.

Jim Gledden, hackdriver for the village hotel, and Captain Klews, the one-armed postmaster, gazed with undisguised curiosity after the disappearing car into which Grannell had hurried his niece.

"Them two look near enough alike to be father and daughter," Jim declared.

"How'd you make that out? Grannell's colder'n a fish since he's got so rich, an' I see with one eye that that girl's got what you'd call magnetism, an' it's a gift of the gods, I reckon," Klews returned.

"Well, you say there's been no end of letters between 'em, and he begun it," Jim Gledden insisted.

"When Sam Grannell begins things whose benefit is he contendin' for, his'n, or somebody else's?" the postmaster retorted, flinging the lean mail bag into the empty hack. "He's let that niece of his'n go homeless for years. Him a widower and childless, and getting well off steady. Just payin' board somewhere for a relative ain't nothin' but cheap charity towards your own flesh an' blood. He's working out some scheme of his own now. You know that's his brand of human kindness."

Klews looked at the little dust cloud receding down the long level highway, and a shrewd twinkle in the gossipy old fellow's eyes told that he had an opinion of his own about things. Edith Grannell's coming became his special grievance hence forth; while, according to the custom of the two to differ, Jim Gledden espoused her cause and made it his own.

Meanwhile, as Samson Grannell, with his niece, sped out toward the open country he was carefully bridging over the years that lay between the little girl whom he had known and this charming self-poised young lady for whom he found himself unprepared. It is so difficult in one's mind to let children grow up.

"I suppose you are glad to be through with school. Did you have a big enough check for your commencement?" he asked.

"I've never needed for anything that money could get," Edith replied, "and I want to pay you for your generosity, for I can earn my living and take care of myself now."

The village postmaster was right when he declared that "Samson Grannell was colder'n a fish." His face was expressionless now as he broke in:

"If you owe me anything it is to do what I want you to do."

"I'll be glad to do anything I can for you," Edith declared with a shining light in her gray eyes.

She was not thinking of the heart-hungry years wherein he had been to her only a name on a bank draft, yet a half-conscious query rose in her mind as to the full extent of such an obligation.

"Then don't speak about earning your living unless you want to offend me. We'll settle that now."

The set lines of Grannell's mouth told that he had clinched a bargain, while the little up-curve of Edith's red lips hinted at another mind than his. But he could not see that then.

"Has the country changed much?" he questioned as indication that that incident was closed.

"Everything seems changed," Edith replied. "The old open prairie is one great wheat field now, and there are no trails left, only straight roads. Are they all like this?"

"Most of them. We follow section lines now. There's only one old fellow left to freeze out, and then the whole country will be straight-cut as a checker board," her uncle replied.

"I like the trails best, maybe because I remember them best," Edith commented.

"We are going a long distance out of our way this morning. I have business with a man out here if I can find him at home. But this wheat is worth looking at anyhow."

As they made a turn in the road Grannell pointed toward a stretch of tender young wheat. Beyond it looming up from the floor of the prairies was Pawnee Rock, a great stone outcrop for whose abrupt upheaval some old volcano must have stoked its fires in the forgotten aeons of time. Sloping gently on one side from a faint swell, dim outline of a prehistoric river bank, it breaks on the other in a sheer stone cliff, isolated and majestic. Like the sphinx of the desert it sits, looking out across the level plains, and the winding foolishness of the Arkansas river forever pushing its way aimlessly about. Just now the bronze front made a splash of rich warmth above the vivid green at its base, while the gray crest softened into the blue and pearl of the sky above it.

"Oh, wonderful!" Edith cried. "Don't you wish that was on your ranch, Uncle Samson?"

"What? The rock? There was never any wheat raised on it, nor anything else, but h —" he caught himself. "No, I don't want it. Every old plainsman has his tale of horror to tell about that rock. It's the corner stone of all the tragedies of the Plains. They were all built on it or about it. We've quit building on things like that now. Our best security is a good bank security."

A horse and rider suddenly stood outlined on the very edge of the bluff, making a statuesque figure against the skyline. A black horse always has the advantage of color, but this one had beauty of form also, while its rider sat firm as a cavalry man, looking out across the landscape, unconscious of the heroic picture he and his horse were making.

With the splendid features of the scene before her, the words of the man beside her seemed sordid to Edith. For one long minute she gazed upward as one who turns from weakness to strength, and the shadow in her gray eyes was like the shadow of the cloud sweeping across the wheat fields.

Then she said with a smile:

"There's no tragedy about that, and it seems to belong up there. Is it set just for our benefit?"

"That's a young neighbor of mine. He is the most popular fellow in the wheat belt according to what Captain Klews and Jim Gledden, official gossips, were saying down at the station this morning. They say that all the girls are crazy about him, but it's a dead certainty he'll marry some rich girl, or one with prospects of money, or he wouldn't be his father's son. He was always a quiet sort of boy, and generally keeps you guessing." Grannell's expressionless face may have changed a trifle as he added, "He'll be a big ranch owner one of these days. He is an only son, and his mother is a widow, one of those women who is set in her ways. I hope you will get acquainted with him soon."

There was a dangerous light in the girl's eyes, but her mouth was forcibly demure as she replied:

"I'm afraid I'm not in his class. He sounds like a cad from this distance. I suppose he is a crushing flirt, too."

"Oh, a fellow in his position, popular with everybody, is bound to be more or less of that, I suppose. It seems to make life interesting, but they get over it." Grannell was not quite sure of his ground.

"And what is the name of the young wheat-belt prince?" Edith asked.

"Homer Helm. You may remember him."

Grannell was looking down the straight road before him, as if he were looking down the years of time. Edith's head drooped a little, for she was thinking back to one sweet day when her only playmate, a freckle-faced little boy with big dark eyes, a boy two years her senior but not nearly so tall as herself, had come for a last play with her. The pink deepened on her cheek as she remembered that he had kissed her good-bye, the only good-bye kiss that had been given her when she left the West. That little boy was Homer Helm, and the memory of that good-bye kiss had been a sacred possession in the poverty of a loveless childhood. To her mind he had never grown up, but was still the little boy of that far-off day, and she wanted to keep him so.

It was almost noon before the two reached the end of their journey. At the crest of a prairie swell a strip of woodland with a bit of open pasture lying beyond came suddenly to view. It was carefully fenced along its irregular outline, save for a bit of grove opening on the roadway.

Down the slope of this swell from which almost every foot of the Grannell ranch might be seen, the stiff, sunny road gave place to a winding way under trees green with May leafage. Here and there a bit of stone outcrop put in a picturesque touch, and at the bottom of the slope a little stream offered that rare thing in Kansas, a real rock-bottom ford. It was such a spot as calls up to the newcomer tender memories of clear brooks in eastern woodlands. Grannell shut off his engine and paused awhile where the trees threw their cool shadows across the way.

"I don't remember this part of the road," Edith said, half-conscious of its appeal. "Is it put here to make folks homesick?"

"We didn't come this way in the old days," her uncle replied. "The Grannell ranch and the Helm ranch hadn't extended their boundaries so far and gathered in so much of this ground then. I always stop here to be sure my tires are all right before I try that hill down to the ford; or to look at the ranch over there in the sunshine; or just from force of habit, maybe. You know habits tighten on us as we get by forty-five."

Edith looked pensively down the cool length of road invitingly comfortable after the straight, unshaded highway. There was no voice in the air of that May morning to tell her that this was a battle ground for a struggle in which she was to have no small part.

"It is a good place to rest in. I hope it will always be here," she said thoughtfully.

"It's useless to hope that," Grannell declared. "It's the last of the trails, and Noel Waverly, the old sissy who owns the ground, won't give up to have it changed; so the road winds down here, crooked as a snake's track, to the ford. But we'll burn him out before long. He's cut off on one side now. Some of these days we'll shut up this road, and bridge the creek straight ahead, leaving him with no outlet. The county commissioners have tried several times to put a bridge down there, but I've fought it every time, pending the changes bound to come. They'll try to get one through this fall, but I'll see to it that it's only a cheap temporary affair. Waverly is a stubborn fellow, the last of the old plainsmen; still living in mind, back in the days of the Santa Fe Trail. He loves a cart and oxen yet, and he wouldn't trade a stout old pony of his, that he calls 'Kit Carson,' for the finest touring car ever turned out. But his time's coming."

"Who will bring it to him?" Edith inquired.

"Oh, the fellow you saw up on Pawnee Rock has the biggest grip. But we'll all help him. We've quit living in the fifties out here; we are in the march of the twentieth century."

Suddenly there came to Edith the memory of long summer Sabbath afternoons with the same little freckle-faced, brown-eyed boy again. There was a plain home under big cottonwood trees, with a gray-bearded man on the doorstep telling stories of Indians and wagon trains, of blazing heat, and no water nearer than the sand-baked Arkansas river, of scalpings, and

14

arrow-wounds, and miraculous rescues for beautiful women, till the shadows lengthened, and the little girl and boy trotted home, hand clutched in hand, half afraid of a Pawnee raid out of yellow wheat stubble, or the war whoop of the Cheyennes from the brown grasses.

But the memory vanished as Edith caught sight of a blue sunbonnet pushed back from a tangle of frowzy golden curls, and a little round face, pink as a peach blossom, with big blue eyes staring at her from a thin screen of bushes beside the road.

To see the child shut in with brown grasses and gray shrubbery, with the shimmer of overhead green and the still shadowy valley behind her, was like finding a living picture in a tarnished old frame. When she found herself discovered the little one who had been watching the auto mobile and listening to all that had been said, disappeared in a thick clump of picturesque greenery a little distance from the road.

"Whose child is that?" Edith asked.

"That is little Faith Clover, Noel Waverly's grandchild, the old cuss who won't give up this crooked trail for a decent road. He wouldn't put her into an orphan asylum. When a man is tied to his home like that he knocks the corner stone out from under his prosperity — and prosperity is the corner stone of life with us. And besides, the youngster didn't need him. Anybody can take care of a child. He was a hard-headed, hard-fisted fighter in his younger years. Never asked nor gave quarter to anybody. But that child has made a change in him. Another spurt now and we'll be at the ranch. There's a short cut by the footpath up from the ford, but it's a good half mile by the road."

Grannell's tone changed with the last sentence as he gripped the steering wheel and sent the car forward with an easy swing.

As for Edith she was beginning already to understand why for twelve years she had known her uncle only as a name on a bank draft, and she was glad that the fair-haired little orphan who had cuddled down in the bushes, behind them would never feel the loneliness she had felt.

Samson Grannell's commodious farm house, with all the modern equipments of a city dwelling, carried a welcome to all who were invited within its doors (Grannell never invited those who were not welcome), and its most hospitable offerings were awaiting the coming of Edith Grannell.

After their lunch together her uncle said: "I'm going to leave you alone here to get yourself adjusted. I shall be busy all this afternoon. By the way, what is your favorite pastime?"

"I've wanted to ride horses ever since I was here years ago. I'm not one bit afraid, and I'm sure I could learn easily," Edith replied.

She did not see the gleam of approval in Grannell's eyes, nor the lines of satisfaction settling about his lips as he left her. Evidently things were working to his liking.

Late that afternoon as she came out to the veranda, Edith caught sight of a handsome cream-colored horse being led by someone down the driveway toward the barns.

"I wonder whose horse that is," she thought, as it disappeared. Then her mind ran into other lines.

"Everything is interesting here. Uncle Samson most of all. He is literally married to money and to having his own way. I can see that already. He doesn't seem to want me to feel my obligation to him but he says I owe it to him to do what he wants me to do. That's all right, Uncle Samson, up to a point. If it's lazy living off a rich uncle when this visit's over, there'll be two Grannells with two minds."

The girl was so bewitchingly pretty with the beauty of one born to ease, coupled with the charm of one who is wholesomely self-dependent, that she might well have broken a harder will than Samson Grannell's.

"He says I'll offend him if I speak of earning my own living. How does he think I can live then? Maybe he thinks I could capture that popular snob who is so sought after, but who must have a rich wife or a girl with 'prospects.' I have 'prospects' — plenty of them. They are my stock in trade. I wouldn't have him nor his to-be heritage," she added half aloud with a scorn in her eyes, and a curl of her lips. "But if he comes trying to impress me with his importance I can play the game out for the fun of it. That's not the little Homer Helm I used to know, though."

A sadness followed the scorn, and she resolved not to think of him again. But for all her resolves the figure of the horse and rider on the verge of the bluff came back to her all that day, and her dreams that night were all of a little playmate, hardly so tall as her shoulder, suddenly standing like a giant on the edge of a high place like the gray edge of Pawnee Rock.

II

God took care to hide that country till He judged His
    people ready,
Then He chose me for His Whisper, and I've found it,
    and it's yours!
                    — Kipling.

IN the twilight of this May day little Faith
Clover sat beside her grandfather watching the
afterglow of sunset through the cottonwood trees. Old
Noel Waverly called his home "The Shadows." Forty
years before, there had been here only a few bushes
growing along a dry draw in the prairie; today a
veritable woodland followed the windings of the
creek. But the trees had been of Noel's planting. His
hands had brought water to them in their early
struggle for a footing. Tenderly he had guarded them
against roving stock and drouth and prairie fire until
the years when, tall, and green, and strong, they
protected him from the heat and moved the heavens
to more generous rainfall in the day of drouth.

The old plainsman had seen the passing out of
the prairie wilderness and the incoming of twentieth
century progress. He had seen, too, the passing out of
wife and children; had seen his once big cattle range
dwindle to a few acres. And now, with the snows of
seventy-five winters on his head, he was ranchman
(in a small way), gardener, and housekeeper, as well

as father, mother, and companion to his little grandchild, the last of the Waverly blood he should ever know. Withal, he was hale and rugged beyond the strength of many younger men, and, with the wisdom of experience, acute to read men's motives and forecast results.

Faith's playground was in the open woodland between the house and the road; here because she was companionless and alone, she dwelt in an imaginary realm which, like all children of normal minds, she peopled to suit her fancy.

"Tell me the story, Dando." Faith was almost eight years old, but she still clung to her baby name for her grandfather. Nestling against his side tonight, she cuddled down to listen.

"It's just the same old tale, Faith. You tell me one," her grandfather replied.

"You tell me first," Faith insisted.

"Well, once on a time there was an old man and his daughter and two plainsmen on Pawnee Rock waiting for a wagon train from the fort to come along. The old man and the younger ones went down to the river for water — and left the girl up there alone. And a young scout was away on the prairies at sunset, and the Indians surprised him. They were Comanches on the warpath, and he rode and rode."

"To Pawnee Rock?" Faith asked eagerly.

"Yes, toward it, but the Indians were gaining on him, and his pony stumbled into a prairie dog's hole, it must have been, and fell, breaking its leg."

"And then, what?" Faith questioned eagerly.

"Then he ran, and ran on foot toward the rock. But the arrows whizzed after him and he would have perished in its shadow only suddenly —"

"What?" Faith's blue eyes shone like stars in the twilight.

"Suddenly a rifle shot right over his head hit the nearest Indian, and another, and another, all coming from the top of the rock. The young girl, oh, such a pretty girl, with big blue eyes, and golden hair — her name was Mary." Noel Waverly's voice was low and tender.

"That was my grandmamma, Dando, and she saved you that evening. And she said she'd be my grandmamma for you always and always. I wasn't here then, but that didn't make no difference to her, and what else?"

"Nothing else." The voice was still tender.

"You learned to love my grandmamma on Pawnee Rock."

"And I loved her always — love her now," the old man said softly.

"Do folks that love on Pawnee Rock love always and always?" Faith asked.

"Always and always," Noel Waverly replied.

"Is Pawnee Rock very far away?" the little one questioned.

"Not very far when you go in a gasoline outfit, but a good long way for our old Kit Carson to trot. I'll take you there some time — you little shut-in child," he added under his breath, "so innocent of the world outside of this tiny place, so wonderful in the world of your imagination."

"Then I'll make my people live on Pawnee Rock," the little girl declared.

"Your people?"

"Yes, all my beautiful people. They are really truly people," Faith explained. "There's nobody else to play with, and I can make them all so pretty, and good, or bad, just like I want them."

"Oh, you little dreamer!" her grandfather said, softly stroking her tangled curls. "You are a lonely child."

"No, I'm not, Dando. I have my brave young scout and my beautiful girl whenever I want them. I saw her today. Oh, I was going to tell you a story."

"I'm listening," the old man said.

"Well, I was down in the fairies' bush by the old Santa Fe Trail where I play like it crosses the big Missouri river, and a great wagon train and sixty yokes of oxens, all full of people came by, and they had to run and hide in the woods for they thought the Pawnees were coming. But it wasn't. It was a big automobile and a beautiful lady, enough to be a grandmamma, was in it, and a big man. I think he was an Indian. They stopped a long time in the shade right by my castle, you know, and I heard them talking. The big man said 'Noel Waverly is an old sissy and — and — crooked as a snake's track,' and he said 'I'll burn him up and cut off one side. He's an old cuss.' That's what he said. But the lady was just as sweet as if I'd made her."

"Oh, you strange little romance-maker! Faith, how much of this is really true?" Waverly asked.

"All of it, Dando," Faith answered gravely.

"No, you are making up part of it," her grandfather insisted.

"Which part?" Faith asked.

The evening shadows were too deep to catch the twinkle in her roguish eyes.

"Why, the man isn't an Indian. He is Samson Grannell. He is trying to get Mrs. Helm and her son to shut up our road and force us to sell this little place to him and Mrs. Helm so they can run section-line roads, and cut down all our trees and straighten the creek and make a great wheat field of this beautiful grove your grandmamma loved."

"Don't let him do it, Dando," Faith urged.

"I never will." Noel Waverly set his jaws sternly. He was a stubborn man. Only stubborn men, his kind of men, could have conquered the Plains and made the wheat belt possible. "He's got some scheme afoot now. Maybe that's why he sent for this girl to come out here."

"Maybe there will be a lover for her like the pretty girl with the rifle," Faith suggested. And then the tired little head drooped against the old man's arm, and the busy brain was still in slumber.

Noel Waverly sat in the shadowy silence long after Faith had gone to sleep.

"I'm an old man, now," he mused, half aloud. "Nearly all my land is gone. The big Helm ranch and the big Grannell ranch are swallowing up what I used to call mine. I wasn't a fortune builder. I cut sod for other men to build on. And now all that's left to me is a few head of stock, a garden, and a truck patch, and this strip of woodland pasture following the winding of the creek so many rods on either side — less than seventy acres across the last quarter of it — this woodland that I planted, 'The Shadows' that Mary loved. I've kept it with its crooked bounds fenced and marked in memory of her. What difference does it make that the boundaries are curves instead of section lines? The rivers wind in and out, the prairies ripple like waves of the sea, the sky is a dome. You can't straighten the rainbow. Life is made up of curves, too — lines of beauty, as well as sharp angles of fact. And we were so happy here, Mary and I, for we loved each other. You may buy acres and acres of wheat land with money and you may build a fine house with money, but 'the life is more than meat, and the body than raiment,' and the corner stone of a home is love."

Then the old man stiffened in his chair and his face grew stern.

"I remember when Grannell was poor enough, him and his wife, living in a little three-roomed house out on the prairie. She died early. Maybe if he'd put the real corner stone under that little three-roomed house she might have lived. Now he's a graspin' widower whose only god is money. Prosperity does that for some men. He's shut me in on his side of the ranch. And he knows that Isabel Helm holds the mortgage on my place." The old man's face was gray with the shadow of calamity. "That mortgage was due thirty days ago. I wonder if Grannell knows that. Of course he does. And it's hard sleddin' even to pay interest. But she won't foreclose on me, nor shut up my road out of here as long as she has the say about things. Homer gets everything in his name when he marries. I wonder what he'll do. He's a quiet boy and nobody knows what he thinks."

The Corner Stone

A new thought leaped up in Waverly's mind.

"Grannell's up to some scheme, or he'd never have sent for that niece of his to come back now." He stroked the sleeping child's golden hair with a loving hand. "Poor little Faith! You've had somebody to love you always, while that little girl has lived among strangers till now. Now! Well, I know Grannell's breed. He wants to freeze me out of 'The Shadows,' and he'll never stop till he's tried every means. I believe I can see the beginning of the end in this move. But I won't give up yet."

In spite of his burdened mind, there was a spark of the old-time daring in Noel Waverly's eyes as if he sniffed a new danger of the Plains that he must outwit.

III

And our pathway wound through the fields of wheat;
Narrow that path and rough the way,
But he was near, and the birds sang true,
And the stars came out in the twilight gray;
    Oh! it was sweet in the evening time!

LITTLE Faith Clover was in Clover Castle, a cunning bower, which Nature and her grandfather's loving hands had wrought for her in the grove near the road. Here, unseen herself, she could see her old Santa Fe Trail, and her Missouri river (the rock-bottomed ford), the Indian tepees in the distance where the silos on the Grannell ranch stood up tall and white, and even Pawnee Rock — the red roof of the big Helm cattle barns. Nobody passing up or down the trail escaped her eyes, and she made a story for each one. The isolated child had, perforce, to build a world of her own, and she interwove the seen and unseen so closely that she herself could not say which was real and which only fancy.

Faith was giving a tea party for her doll, a poor enough rag affair, but endowed with all beauty and charm by the child's ready imagination; and forty other doll guests were beginning to arrive from Japan and London and Larned, Kansas, when a real prince came riding out of fairyland in search of a princess. So Faith dropped the social function, to make a princess for him. It was so like a real story that Faith had no trouble "fixing the corners," as she phrased it, when she built romances out of "dream stuff" only.

Homer Helm riding up the Waverly line to look after the fences, came whistling along the shady bound of the wheat field.

He was a stalwart young fellow, six feet in height with physique to match. His face had the ruddy tinge of outdoor country life, not the hard brown of the farm drudge, for he was a master, not a servant, of the soil.

"Poor old Waverly!" he muttered, as he slid from his horse.

Slipping the rein over his arm, he began to stiffen up a weak spot in the fence with the hatchet he carried.

As he stooped to his task, his horse suddenly reared, jerking the rein on his master's arm.

"Ho, Blackstone! what's the matter now?" he spoke quietly.

"It's the princess coming. I didn't have to make her, she is real," Faith Clover exclaimed excitedly behind the bushes. But Homer did not hear her. Neither did the princess.

Edith Grannell was coming up the steep slope from the creek, carrying a basket of wild flowers and a little white linen jacket that matched the white linen dress she wore. Bareheaded, with her rich brown hair catching the glint of the sunlight in its heavy fold, and her eyes with the startled look in them, she was wondrously handsome just now. Any young prince's heart would beat faster at sight of her.

Ordinarily, Homer Helm would have lifted his hat and turned away. From his side of the equation he was no ladies' man. He had always been a quiet boy with a dignity that was misjudged shyness. Yet since he had come home from college to manage his mother's ranch he had been the lion of the community. He was young and handsome after the strong, rugged type of manly good looks; reserved, but, to those who knew him well, of innately winning manners.

He was as yet only the representative of his mother. Isabel Helm was a strong-minded quiet woman, of kindly disposition, and strangely handsome because of her dark eyes and the pretty pink flush forever coming and going on her cheeks.

At this unlooked for meeting Edith Grannell was the first to speak.

"I beg your pardon, did I frighten your horse?" she asked.

The voice stirred a curious vibration to life in the young man's memory.

"Oh, no! he can always find something to rear up over. He keeps on the lookout for that," Homer replied, conscious that he was staring at this white-robed figure; at the round white arms below the lace at the elbows; at the gold monogram,

at the shapely throat; at the face crowned with lustrous hair, and eyes the color of cloud-shadows on brown prairie grasses.

"He is very handsome anyhow." Edith looked admiringly at Blackstone and turned to pass on her way.

Then came that strange phenomenon of youth. Passing around the corner of the Helm and Waverly fences, Homer momentarily blocked her way. He had no idea who she might be, but he did not want to end the interview here.

"Do you like horses?" he asked.

"Better than anything else," Edith replied. "If I want to take the shortest cut from the cradle to the grave, with fewest stop-over privileges, I'll take a touring car, but when I want to live and see the life about me, I prefer a thoroughbred."

There was a bran-new seven passenger beauty in a new garage beyond the red cattle barns, and Homer had never known a girl before who didn't prefer a car to any other vehicle. Yet here was one who smiled at him, but not on him, coolly declaring her preference for a thoroughbred roadster. Unconsciously this girl was cutting his self-complacency, too, but she was none the less interesting for that.

"I am going to have a splendid cream-colored saddle-horse as soon as it is trained," Edith went on. "Its name is White Rock. I think there is something of the Pawnee Indian about me, for I love to ride. Do you think horses are so very dangerous for women to manage? "

In spite of her prejudice against the grown-up Homer Helm, Edith was finding it easy to talk to him.

Homer looked at Blackstone to hide his surprise, for he was the owner of the cream-colored horse in question.

"I am sure White Rock is not. I am selling him to the Grannell ranch myself, and I'm training him now. I didn't know who it was for. Samson Grannell bargained for him a week ago, if I'd get him trained fit for a woman's hand. I supposed he had some good buyer, and he was getting a commission."

"Tell me all about his traits and tricks — the horse's I mean; then it won't take so long for me to get to ride him."

"Won't you sit down?"

Homer threw Blackstone's rein over the fence post with the words, and the two sat down opposite each other on a low rock outcrop.

"They are over the line into my fairy land; they belong to me," little Faith Clover declared, her big eyes fastened on the two unconscious of her presence.

Above them the leafy branches swayed gently in the breezes of May. Before them the wheat rippled softly up to the curving bound of "The Shadows." Behind them the wooded valley rested in the quiet of the early summer afternoon. And far overhead hung the great fathomless arch of the heavens with clouds of pearl drifting far away in its dreamy azure depths.

"I am Miss Grannell, Samson Grannell's niece. I have come here to visit for the summer," Edith explained, reverting gracefully to conventional demands.

Everything was changed with this simple introduction. Heretofore Homer Helm had had little interest, except business interest, in Samson Grannell or his relatives.

"I am glad you are here." Homer knew he was getting on awkwardly, for his first impulse was to rise and shake hands. "I am Homer Helm. Our ranch joins Grannell's, except where this little wiggle of grove and pasture along the creek divides us. It is a pretty place, unprofitable though for all of us, and a losing game for old man Waverly. He's mortgaged to the limit."

Big, and handsome, and capable to do or to undo, the speaker appeared as he said this. Edith recalled what her uncle had said about the disastrous future awaiting Noel Waverly. It was not the sun shine but the shadow that came into her gray eyes, with Homer's words.

"Tell me about this old Noel Waverly. We can talk of White Rock afterward," she urged.

It was delicious to hear her speak so familiarly of the things so common to him. It seemed to make her presence permanent. He had been feeling from the first moment of the interview that this was the only time they would ever talk together.

"I've known him all my life. He used to tell me tales of the Plains — he was a freighter in the early days — and of old Pawnee Rock. Many a summer afternoon I've listened to his stories, till I was afraid to go home."

Homer Helm paused. The red color surged into his face, then ebbed away, leaving it very pale.

"Are you Edith, the little girl I used to know, who went away so long ago?" he asked.

Something in his deep voice was appealing.

"Yes, I am Edith who went away so long ago."

For one long moment they looked at each other and neither could guess the other's thoughts.

I remember that you were freckled and wore a pink sunbonnet on the back of your neck," Homer declared at length, chopping at a bush with his hatchet.

"I remember that you were not nearly so tall as I, and that you always had a finger tied up with a more or less sanitary looking rag," Edith answered.

Homer laughed and looked at his large shapely hands.

"I was an unfortunate cuss," he said. "I'm still that way. I broke an arm before I was fourteen, and a leg on the college gridiron. I broke my head in a race at the county fair. I've broken a good many of the ten commandments, and about everything else, except my heart — and it's not altogether immune. Just now I'm breaking a deliciously vicious colt for Mr. Samson Grannell; and I may even try to break into good society some time."

"Breakers ahead! Do all the young men out here have as much energy as you have?" Edith inquired.

Homer wondered if she was covertly ridiculing him and his kind, holding the social life of the wheat belt in a sort of contempt.

"We are a fairly energetic lot out here," he answered with seeming carelessness. "Is that bad form in the East? We get as far as the universities ourselves sometimes. Some of us can expand the binomial theorem real fast; and we can appreciate a Corot sunset even if we do have a superior article in the real thing out here."

"Astonishing!" Edith declared looking away, and keeping down a smile. "It is a good looking country anyhow."

"Oh, the country is a cracker-jack," Homer assured her. "And you'll take to the natives sooner or later. They all do. Have you come out to live, or just to look at us awhile, and then vanish from our view? "

"I suppose he is sounding my 'prospects.' I'll mystify the young gentlemen a bit," Edith thought. Aloud she said: "It all depends on how well you behave. My plans are indefinite. You see if my face won't be my fortune, my hands will have to be, unless — but that's family matter, and uninteresting to anyone else. Tell me about your sociological stratum out here." Edith's eyes were full of a dancing light.

Followed then a grotesque picturing of the impossible in the great rich Kansas wheat belt, all of which Edith pretended seriously to believe, wondering the while at the young man's ability to hide the self-conceit she had attributed to him.

The minutes ran unnoticed; and, although they talked of the wheat belt, of Kansas, and of the West in general, neither one referred again to the days of their childhood together.

The level rays of the sun were striking through the trees when they suddenly remembered themselves.

"I'll walk home with you, if you don't care," Homer said, with a hungering for the interview to continue. And together they followed the winding path, half shadow, half sunshine, between the Waverly woodland and the fields of wheat.

Little Faith Clover in her leafy castle clapped her hands as she looked after them.

"It's real," she murmured. "They are a real story."

IV

I am dreaming again of the golden years
　　That have sped like arrows across the sea;
　　And strange, sweet visions return to me —
And memories sad — too sad for tears —
　　A curious blending of hopes and fears,
　　Once painted by fancy, wild and free.
　　　　　　　　　　— A. W. Macy.

THE path from the Waverly grove to the Grannell home led down the shaded slope to the stepping-stones at the ford of the creek, across a bit of meadow, and through the corner of the orchard to the shady dooryard. Along this path the two young people loitered in the late afternoon, and the way was very pleasant, as the paths of youth should be.

"I hope this will not be our last walk together," Homer said courteously, as they reached the gateway to the shady lawn.

"Thank you, Mr. Helm," Edith began, but her companion broke in.

"Oh, call me Homer. We needn't be formal, need we?"

"Thank you, Mr. Homer," Edith amended. "My name, by the way, is Edith. I'll be glad to walk anywhere till I learn to ride."

"I have a notion I could train White Rock better with you to help me. Will you do it?" Homer asked. "The inspiration just came to me."

"Delighted," Edith ejaculated, "if you have the time to waste on me."

"I'll take the time, and it won't be wasted either. It will be a real missionary work I'm sure. My main occupation on earth is to serve my community, anyhow," Homer replied.

"Oh, I'll have Uncle Samson pay you so much per teach," Edith declared.

"Good! I'll demand full wage, too. But, seriously, when shall we begin?"

"Whenever you are ready to begin seriously," Edith replied, a challenge to mischief in the laughing gray eyes.

"It's a bargain, then, but I warn you it's a good season's work, although well-bred horses learn fast," Homer assured her.

"So do well-bred people. Good-bye, and many thanks."

The laughing gray eyes held a place before Homer Helm's mind as he galloped away toward the big red barns that made a playlike castle, or a playlike Pawnee Rock for Faith Clover.

"She's a girl a fellow can be sure of," he thought, as his mind ran over the whole afternoon again and again. "I wonder what she thinks of me."

What Edith thought she said to her uncle at tea time.

"I met your neighbor, Mr. Helm, today. I think I can understand why he has a reputation for popularity and also why you say he is something of a flirt. He can carry off the part without pretending to do it. He must be all the less worthy down underneath the pretense. He is going to teach me to ride this summer, but I promise now, Uncle Samson, I'll not let my scalp be added to his collection of trophies." Edith spoke lightly, too busy with thoughts of the afternoon to notice her uncle's long silence.

If Samson Grannell had broken that silence he would have said:

"What you think and what Homer Helm thinks is nothing to me. I have one plan for these two ranches, one dream to be fulfilled, and you two must bring it about. I shall play my game carefully, and I never lose."

Late that evening Homer Helm sat in his little runabout car before the door of the village postoffice, waiting for Captain Klews to bring his mail. A trip to the postoffice every evening was a part of the routine of the Helm household, although the rural mail route included the Helm ranch in its course every forenoon. Market quotations on stock and grain were too important to the young manager to be delayed by slow delivery of morning papers.

"Let your clerk run the office and I'll give you a turn around town," Homer called to the postmaster.

"Coming in a minute. Don't take the trouble to get out," the old Captain called cheerily from behind the glass box-sections of the postoffice.

"It would break the old gossip's heart not to get out here and sit in the car awhile and tell me the latest stories going. Who says women have a monopoly on busy body business, anyhow?" Homer mused as he lounged back in his seat.

"Here's your mail — Kansas City an' Topeky papers, an' your farm journals."

Captain Klews gave Homer the mail and sat down on the comfortable cushions with a sigh of satisfaction.

"We didn't have none of these here easy seatin's when I was a young man and your pa was helpin' to take the three-quarters that was left of me off'n the battlefield, an' me a-bleedin' to death slow. An' your pa never left me —"

Evidently this was a well-known story, for Homer, smiling kindly, interrupted:

"That's all right. You've about stopped bleeding now. Tell me the news."

Captain Klew's eyes twinkled, for he was a born gossip.

"Say, d'you hear about your new neighbor up there, Sam Grannell's niece? "

"No. What's to hear? " Homer was looking at his speedometer as if it were a Chinese puzzle.

"Why, they're tellin' she's come out here to marry some rich feller. Seems strange they'd say that about her knowin' how little store Sam sets by riches. You know he sent for her to come. He's always paid her bills, but never invited her out here till now. He couldn't be aggin' her on in this, d'you reckon?"

Klews laughed boisterously and winked knowingly at Homer who was still engrossed with the speedometer.

"An' you hadn't heard? Course you'd be the last one to hear it." This with a sly dig in the young man's side. "Maybe she's playin' into Grannell's hand, an' maybe it's gossip. She ain't got an Eastern chap, one of them snobs, on the string, too, I should hope. I don't pay much attention to anything I hear though. How's your ma?"

"No, you don't pay much attention, that's a fact," Homer answered drily. "Mother is very well, except a little shortness of breath, now and then, when she's excited."

"She'd better not get excited. Them pink cheeks of hers ain't real natural in a middle-aged woman."

"They surely aren't artificial," Homer said with a smile.

"She's a mighty good-lookin' woman anyhow. Well, here we are. How quick you can git round town and back in one of these fire wagons. You don't have to go right out home, do you?"

"I forgot about this being the dark of the moon, and my lights are bad. I must be going."

As he leaned across to open the door for the crippled man, Klews said in a low voice:

"Homer, don't let no girl do you, specially one of Sam Grannell's backin'. Don't do it. I've knowed you so long I'd hate to see that."

There was so much of genuine affection in the old man's voice that Homer patted the armless shoulder as he helped the postmaster from the car.

The Corner Stone

There was no moon, no star, no light for Homer Helm on that homeward ride.

"I'm in for a horse-training stunt anyhow," he muttered as he sent his runabout on at a furious rate. "What difference does it make if she does want a rich husband, or whether one or a dozen 'Eastern snobs,' as old Cap. Klews calls them, has the inside track. She's not like any other girl I ever knew. If she wants to play a mere season's game out in the wheat belt, I'm her man. And we'll run one jolly race for one jolly summer anyhow. The fall can take care of itself. If it's money she's after, I haven't it, that's all. I'm Isabel Helm's hired boy and she won't care for me. And I couldn't care for her. So the horseback riders will ride on and on, and the gossips may go to — the fellow who will get 'em all without my sending.

"I used to look up to her when I was a little lonely boy long ago. Somehow, I've kept thinking I'd always look up to her if we ever met again. And now I know I've always been wanting to meet her again. The thing has sort of grown up with me as I grew. Just a boy's boyish dream, that's all. And she is a real live worth-while girl — damn a gossip!" He growled vehemently, as he leaned down and pressed the electric button below the seat.

"I may as well turn on the lights now. Lord forgive me for telling Klews that lie about them; I had to get away quick right then. The loving-hearted old scamp would pretty nearly die for me because he was

my father's army comrade — but he couldn't know
—"

The sentence went unfinished in the young
man's mind. The night shadows hid the young face.

Golden Lights
thro'
Purple Haze

V

Who shall say, in the heart of a child,
    Fanciful, joyous, light and free,
    Full of vagueness and mystery,
Pure, and simple, and undefiled,
Never there come, in fancies wild,
    Glimpses of what is yet to be?
              —A. W. Macy.

TO find how Providence can "scatter plenty o'er a smiling land" one must see the great Kansas wheat belt on a banner crop year. Samson Grannell's ranch had never before known such an enormous yield, and the Grannell bank account was increasing in proportion to the harvest returns. Already the owner of the ranch and bank account was planning yet larger profits for the coming season. To such men as Grannell money has only one use — to beget money.

On a summer afternoon in August, the Grannell automobile stopped beside the Waverly grove. The owner and a shrewd-faced man sat in the comfortable shade looking out at the creek and woodsy valley and the few acres of open meadow beyond.

"You get the lay of it? Any civil engineer can do that," Grannell was saying. "The old man's bound to go under anyhow. This thing's not going to hang fire forever, and we may as well be ready to begin on it and not lose any time when the end comes. Now figure this road in, the new shorter road off, the cost of straightening the creek and grading down that rough part. Then there's a little expense in clearing off this growth."

Grannell took off his hat to let the little streak of cool air coming up the valley fan his brow, the man beside him making rapid notes as he talked.

"Say, Sam," the pencil rested and the keen eyes studied Grannell's face. "What's your grudge against the old man? Why not let him hang on here awhile?"

"Look at the profit in wheat lost every year," Grannell returned.

"Do you get it all?" queried his companion.

"I'll control it mainly. Helm and I will square our places. All that triangle down there will be added on to my ground, eventually. All that prevents it being there right now is a woman hanging on to an over-due mortgage instead of foreclosing. But she can't say a word after her son marries. He'll be sole proprietor then. Think of two such fine ranches with a corner chewed off like this between 'em. We've each got five sections, the best wheat land west of

Hutchinson. This measly sixty-six and seven-eighths acres goes zigzagging through here a few rods wide on either side of the creek, marked and fenced in to the inch by an old back number plainsman. Their day has gone by. We are living in a practical age, not an age of imagination. We deal in straight lines, not curves, and you don't find much mushy sentimentalism now-a-days. The corner stone of things in this world is cold cash."

"It's a comfortable place on such a darned hot day as this, anyhow," the other man asserted. "Kind of restful to see a tree like these once in awhile by the road side, and the natural curves of this slope couldn't be beat by a landscape-maker. Honest, Sam, isn't it all just dollars you want?"

Grannell set his jaws sternly.

I've set my heart on it so long I'm never going to give up now till it's done. And I'm not the only common-sense business man around here. Helm knows all this as well as I do. He's a young man of judgment, and he'll show it too when he is head of that ranch one of these days. As to money, isn't it what we all want and need? It's the only thing that talks to me. That's the kind of a man I am."

"Well, by jinks, you weren't always that kind of a man. I knew you back when your wife was living and you were poor. Prosperity's been hard on you, Sam Grannell. I pity you."

Grannell made no response as he stepped from the car to get a better view of the place he was condemning.

"Hold on there. You are spoiling some kid's playhouse," the engineer cried, as Grannell broke down the bushes and kicked aside the vines hiding the view across the upper line of "The Shadows."

Grannell hardly noted the havoc he had wrought in Faith Clover's castle, nor did he see the tragic face and tear-wet eyes of the little girl who bad slipped away just at that minute and stood trembling beyond the fairy bush. What could a practical man of money and might know of castles and fairy bushes and the heart-break their loss would mean to a loving little dreamer of dreams, a part of whose very life they were? He dealt in realities, and wheat land is a very real thing.

It seemed a long time to the shy child, that these two men talked of levels and timber and wheat values, which she could not understand, and of the bad fortune overhanging her beloved "Dando," which she grasped clearly. It was a day of tragedy as real to her as the great tragedies that blight the careers of grown-up children in their larger world.

"Oh, Dando can fix it all right, Faith," Noel Waverly declared that evening, as he caressed the tumbled golden curls and sought to cool the tear-stained face perspiring against his shoulder in an effort to hide its grief. "Don't cry, little sweetheart.

You can make a story out of all this trouble, with a wicked ogre or a Pawnee Indian. I know you can."

Faith looked up brightly. God's love is nowhere sweeter than in the quick mending of little broken hearts.

"I can tell you such a big, big story, Dando, and it's not dream stuff, it's all real — most of it is anyhow," she amended conscientiously.

"It's about a prince and princess," Faith explained. "He came riding up toward my castle on a big black horse, last violet time, 'tending like he was fixing the fence where White Face pushed it to bite the wheat, and just then she came right out of a violet, I mean "— Faith was trying hard to be practical — "she came up from the Missouri river, the creek, you know, Dando, with flowers, and they were both so s'prised. I played they liked each other right away, but they didn't know it. I'm most afraid they don't know it yet," Faith added doubtfully.

"Is that all?" Noel Waverly asked.

"Oh, there's more. And I know, cross my heart, it's all truly, and not dream stuff. They come 'most every day close to my castle. I try not to miss them. They may need me any minute to tell them they love each other. That's my part of the play. Don't laugh, Dando. It's all just my story I make up about them."

Faith put up her hand to cover the old man's mouth.

"She's got a horse named White Rock. And his, the prince's, you know, is Blackstone. Her runcle asked him to go riding with her. I made that up myself. I guess her runcle wants her to marry the prince. I made that up, too. She's poor, you know, and if they do marry, why all the big ranches will be just one big ranch, 'cept this little wiggle of grove and pasture along the creek. That's what the prince calls it. I didn't make that up."

Old Noel gave a start.

"That's that scoundrel's scheme. I knew he was up to some cussedness," he cried.

"Oh, I just made that fit in there about the runcle, you know, cause be said today that when the creek is straight and the land is level and the trees all gone, the two ranches would be square and he'd control it. How could he control it, Dando, less'n she marries the prince? He's his mamma's boy, and don't have to mind her runcle."

Poor old Waverly sat very still while Faith harked back to happier things.

"He's such a beautiful prince. I play like all the ladies love him. But I play like he loves to be with the princess best.

He comes up to the edge of the wheat field when she is under the trees. And I visit with them, and they never know. I play like she is poor like Cinderella and her runcle says money talks. It's going to end all right though, and be happy ever after, just like the story-book stories. But it's so real, Dando, so real."

Faith paused a minute, then she added:

"They are going to Pawnee Rock pretty soon. And you said yourself, Dando, folks who love on Pawnee Rock love always and always. I can't hardly wait for them to come back. But, oh, Dando, my castle's all broke down. How can I visit with them any more, and bow will they know they shall love each other if they don't find out on Pawnee Rock? Maybe," she added with the philosophy of childhood, "maybe though, there'll be a way just made for the story to end. And maybe the runcle won't take away the trees my grandmamma loved, and make it all a wheat field. And everything will be happy ever after. I'd rather have pretty castles, and trees, and my Santa Fe trail, and Pawnee Rock and grandmammas, and love. They are all better than just wheat, Dando?"

"All better, Faith," Noel Waverly said softly. "And some day everybody will be happy ever after."

VI

On Pawnee Rock in the sunshine, where the
    Winds of Promise blow,
A cloud, free and fine as a fancy, veils the
    blue with a milder glow.
O'er the prairie grass its shadow, like a
    gypsy dancer, sways,
Keeping time to the mystic music that the
    pulse of Nature plays;
The purple and cream and amber of a
    hundred thousand flowers
Tint the land like an Aztec mantle, all the
    silent and shining hours.
If there is in the world a nepenthe for the
    heartache the most of us know,
On Pawnee Rock you may find it, where the
    Winds of Promise blow.

IT is the way of some men that the farther they get from boyhood, the stronger is the bold of youthful ideals upon their minds, that with a strange reserve and dignity they hide all the deeper from the sight of men. As Homer Helm, a shy little undersized country boy, grew up to the stature of a stalwart man, certain boy ideals had clung to him and strengthened with his strength. Samson Grannell had said, "Young Helm generally keeps you guessing," but none of his neighbors understood how timidity had grown into reserve and dignity, offset, in this case, by a naturally winning personality.

Now in his fourth summer at home his fine new automobile was jacked up off the cement floor of the new garage, while its owner devoted himself to wheat harvesting; or, as reports ran, too often went horseback riding with Samson Grannell's niece. It kept Jim Gledden and Captain Klews both busy to keep up with the gossip of the day and make due report at train time.

A penniless girl, supported by her uncle must have a purpose in this visit. As to her ever inheriting her uncle's property — that was a problem. Sam Grannell wasn't the kind of man to ever leave anything. If he set his jaw, he'd lug his whole ranch right through the pearly gates in the face of old St. Peter and all the other saints. If ever Klews longed for the lost arm left on the battle field, he longed for it now that he might shake two fists every time he heard the name of Grannell.

As to Edith Grannell, she ought to know that Homer was just flirting because she was the new girl in the neighborhood. He'd marry rich. It was in the Helm blood to add to prosperity. This was the community grievance, nursed and developed by Jim Gledden, who stood up as valiantly for Edith as his old associate fought for Homer Helm.

It happened that from the first day's meeting under the trees in the Waverly woodland, Homer and

Edith, each safeguarded in mind against the other, felt secure in a summer-time association. It could mean nothing more serious at most than the discovery that neither one had been deceived by the other. There was a spice more of zest in the game each was playing, an old, old game anywhere, because of this security; and the playing was a little more reckless because deep down there was a conscious disapproval of it in each mind.

The one strange feature of this good fellowship was that neither one spoke of their childhood days together. Outside of this they were becoming royal chums, taking no further responsibility than the acceptance of the offerings the careless summer days brought to them.

It was only to Faith Clover, the lonely little dreamer watching their coming and going, that they became "playlike" lovers.

On the day of the fall of Faith's castle, Edith had come by the short path through the Grannell fields up to where the grove, sweet with refreshing morning air, invited to an invigorating hour. On the evening before she had lost her monogram pin as she had visited awhile with little Faith, who was playing about under the trees. She might find it, for the grass now lay flat and slick on the hard ground.

And here she had found Homer Helm who had come up early, by chance of course, to figure on the value of forage as a late crop on the stubble next to the woodland.

"This is the best part of the day for me," Edith declared, as they loitered about the edge of the stubble field. "Another hour and the sky will be brass and the fields a furnace."

"Hard on freckles but good for the corn — in the corn belt, I mean. It is a seared land out there, though; a blazin', blisterin', blightin', bloomin' hot country in August It's my native habitat, but I wonder that you stay here," Homer declared.

There was nothing in his face to show what else he was wondering, as he looked at her so refreshingly clean and comfortable in her white morning dress.

The shadows deepened momentarily in the gray eyes.

"My uncle hasn't said I've staid too long yet, but, of course, I am not going to sit here with folded hands always. All summers come to an end, you know."

It would be easy to drift on if summers were endless, but that firm mouth and chin could never belong to a girl with a purposeless life.

"Working for one's living isn't a bad proposition. Help is always scarce out here. You can easily find a job," Homer said lightly, "but this going away is quite another story, even if it is a beastly hot country. Good-byes are even worse than dumb endurance, and traveling less comfortable than staying in the shade."

Did they remember the day on which they had separated once before? Neither looked up at that moment, and Faith Clover (in her castle also, because it was the cool of the morning) wondered why they should stop talking for so long a time.

"Oh, I can stand the heat all right. I'm up by daylight every morning not to miss this delicious hour," Edith said at length.

"Edith, would you like to see the sunrise from Pawnee Rock some morning? The New Jerusalem hasn't anything over it for coloring. Gates of pearl, and foundations garnished with all manner of precious stones and seas of glass mingled with fire. And that's no blasphemy either."

"I wish I might. Is it far away? Uncle Samson and I passed near it on the day I came back to Kansas. We were all the morning getting home." Clear in memory was the picture of it as it bad appeared crowned with the heroic figure on the morning of her coming hither.

"It is not very far if we go in the auto, but it's a glorious horseback ride if you don't mind getting up pretty early for beauty sleepers. Maybe you'd rather go in the car, though."

"And maybe I wouldn't. Some folks don't need beauty sleep, and some are no better looking with it anyhow," Edith declared.

"Well, let's go tomorrow. My goosebone tells me this hot south wind is minded to shift to the north by tomorrow morning. Sometimes a streak of real Colorado weather slips across the prairies for a brief visit in August. Will you be ready to start early?"

"The answer is 'I will,'" Edith replied.

"Then the black charger and the white palfrey will be pawing at your portcullis in the gray light of the morning," Homer responded.

"All right. I must go now. I came up to find a little monogram pin that I think I lost here," Edith said, searching the ground about her feet.

"What was it like?" Homer's finger was on the pin in his pocket, as he asked the question. He had found it and, recognized it as belonging to her before she came up. He hesitated now merely to tease her.

"Oh, it was just a little gold pin of a club of girls I once belonged to. We called ourselves the 'Hope Ever' Club, and the club pin was like this," Edith drew the outline in the dust with a stick.

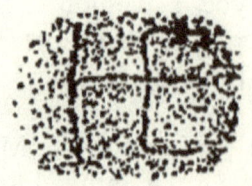

Homer studied the figure. "'H. E.' joined together," he said. "N-no, I don't see it anywhere. I'll help you find it sometime, I hope ever," he added.

It's no great loss," Edith insisted as she started toward home.

"But it might be to somebody," Homer called after her, as he mounted Blackstone. "Remember tomorrow morning at the time St. Peter took for lying about his friends, then we'll be off."

The least-known hour of the twenty-four is the hour of dawn. Yet no other hour is fraught with more beauty, or refreshing sweetness than the dawn of an August morning on the prairies. Whatever the burden in the heat of the day, however stifling the close night shadows, this one hour comes in blessing. The birds twittering sleepily from the leafy coverts of noonday, forget not at early mass to praise God from whom all blessings Sow. And every growing thing — grassblade and flower and shrub and tree — feels the pulse of new strength for the new day.

It was yet too dark to see the road when Homer and Edith started out the next morning, and all the miracle of a new-made day, a miracle as old as the Tuesday morning of creation week, unrolled before them. Black, shapeless shadows in the landscape took form, turned gray, then came to their rightful selves and purposes: The wayside flowers seemed to burst into bloom. And everywhere, from grove and meadow and brown stubble came a wave of music, soft and clear, the morning chant of the birds rippling on, mile after mile, rising at last in one grand chorus of hallelujahs.

Homer and Edith rode slowly at first after the manner of good horsemen. But long before the gray shadows bad lifted, the two horses were swinging in the easy pace of the thoroughbred down the long straight road, their hoofbeats smothered in the soft black dust, until, at length, they mounted the long slope that leads to the brow of Pawnee Rock.

The fresh morning breeze was surging over all the land. The west was a blur, cool green and blue, against a void of distance. Below them the stubble fields, golden-brown in the dawning light, rolled away and away like a vast velvet carpet spread to the very ends of the earth. A filmy curtain hung above the Arkansas river, hiding its level sands and low-growing shrubbery.

Above a horizon of blending purple and scarlet, all the east was one roseate glory shimmering through silvery mist and melting at last far up the sky into an exquisite tracery of mother-of-pearl, until the new born August day was christened in a sunburst of splendor, and the young man and woman standing together watched the world bid good morning to the light.

Oh, this is superb," Edith cried as they stood on the crest of the great volcanic outcrop, and looked over the land awaiting the chrism of a new day.

"Yes, it's worth the effort," Homer's voice was rich and deep as he added, "and I saw a new heaven and a new earth, for the first heaven and the first earth were passed away, and there was no more sea.'

Was it because of the early morning hour, or because of the beauty of the Kansas prairie below them, or because of the uplift of soul that comes to him who stands on high places, or because they were alone together that the dross slipped away, and the fine gold of life remained? A long while they stood silently side by side, a feeling of nearness, of a new understanding of each other holding them both.

As they turned to view the long low swell of land to the northward, a cool wind came sweeping over its crest, bringing the vigor of refreshing in its caress.

"I was waiting for this north breeze. I knew it was coming," Homer declared. "It will be fine for the home run — if we ever have to make it. Let's live awhile by ourselves up here."

"Tell me about this rock, while we are resting," Edith said as they sat down facing the great silent land to the south.

"It used to be ever so much higher. It's been chipped and chopped off for commercial purposes. You know the grip of commercial purposes." Homer checked his tongue, as he remembered Samson Grannell. "It was a landmark on the old Santa Fe Trail, a citadel of the Plains in Noel Waverly's day, a monument to more tragedies than any other one spot in North America. This was the corner stone on which the civilization of the West was builded, a thing to rest on and to fight from.

"There were more Indian fights right here — it got its name from an awful Pawnee battle; more rescuers and refugees have stood on this cliff, the pursuers, and the pursued; more nameless graves and unburied dead in the soil below us. Sometimes it was the white man, and sometimes the red man, who held the fortress. The Indians could see from the top here to old Fort Zarah on the east and Fort Larned on the west. They could count the size of the wagon trains starting out from either place, and when they got to the foot of this bluff somebody perished, for this was the place of sepulchre."

Edith shivered as she tried to picture it all.

"Oh, don't be afraid. The danger passed with the passing of old Noel Waverly's breed. It isn't peril so much as prosperity that threatens some of us. By the way, what was it you said yesterday about going away? Aren't you having a good time here?" As he spoke Homer was cutting some lines on the rock beside him, at the risk of ruining his pocket-knife.

"I said nothing very definite, and I am having a good time," Edith replied. "All this is a matter yet to be settled between Uncle Samson and myself. You said this rock was the corner stone of civilization in the West — a thing to rest on and to fight from. Uncle Samson and I do not

always agree on what is the real corner stone of life — to rest on and fight from. But that's future history. Let's go back to tradition. I saw you on the top of this rock on the morning I came to Kansas."

"You did?" Homer ejaculated in surprise. Then he added, with pretended sincerity, "Yes, I was out looking for you. What did you think it was up here?"

"I thought it was a man." Edith had almost said "strength as matched against the man beside me," but she added: "I thought it had grown quite a little. Do you remember some of the Indian stories we used to listen to until we were afraid to go home, or have you forgotten them?"

Edith asked the questions to hide her confusion for she had never meant to refer to the old days until Homer himself should recall them.

The Corner Stone

"I've never forgotten anything of those old days — and I never want to forget."

Homer's eyes were still on the rock he was carving, but there was a new note in his voice, a note of sadness, as if speaking of the beloved dead. "And since I haven't forgotten anything, I still remember the day you went away and left a little boy so lonely."

He put one hand lightly on her shoulder for a moment, as they suddenly rose to their feet.

The horses, weary from the long journey at an hour when a horse by nature rests, stood quietly by with drooping heads.

No sounds came from the plains below. The August morning was superb in its silence. And they were together on Pawnee Rock. In that moment the lost years were bridged over. Samson Grannell's well-planned scheme for his own profit, the mutual misjudgment of character forced upon these two by greed and jealousy and circumstance, the cheapness of a game of mutual pretense and mutual deception — all fell away in the presence of the sweet air that plays about the brow of Pawnee Rock and the broad grandeur of the earth and the fulness thereof that lies in lengths of fruitful beauty about its base. And yet, neither this man nor this woman, each with a sacred memory of a by-gone day, cherished by strange circumstances through all the succeeding days, could dare to believe that what had grown in precious value to one meant more than one of a thousand childhood memories to the other.

Edith looked up, the light of the morning in her gray eyes; but Homer, who was staring down at the lines he had been cutting on the rock, lost their illuminating ray.

"Edith, what was it that little monogram pin that you lost stood for?" he asked in a changed voice.

"Hope ever," she replied carelessly.

"Was it anything like these lines here?"

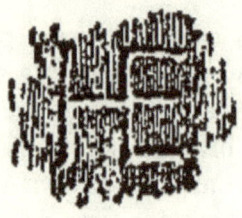

Edith saw the crude marking on the face of the rock at his feet.

"Yes, just like that," she said.

"Too bad to lose it. It might stand for a good many things besides your motto. I like the meaning and the design. Shall we come back here sometime and see if the symbol has disappeared, too, like the thing it stands for? It is a good place to tie to when things get mixed up down on the prairie. Would you care to come back again with me?"

There was a longing in the young man's brown eyes, and a sort of weariness in his motion as he turned to the waiting horses. It was good to be up here with Edith as he would have her be, free from mercenary suggestion. Up here he could never doubt her sincerity, her womanliness. He was tired and ashamed of the game he had been playing. The summer was coming to an end. Then Edith would be going away. That was to be the end of everything.

"Would you care to come back here for a sunset some evening with me?" he asked again, as he led White Rock aside for her to mount.

An eager longing possessed Edith to believe in him fully at that moment, and a bitter resentment against her uncle's estimate of him as a flirt and a fortune getter filled her heart.

"When you want me to come again, you may tell me so," she answered as she caught the bridle rein.

"Are you really going away at the end of the summer?" Homer queried as he helped her to her saddle and stood looking up at her, one hand resting on White Rock's creamy mane.

He did not want the summer to end if she said yes. Yet he hoped with all his heart she would say it.

It would so exalt her above the cheap gossip that he hated.

A wave of deeper pink swept the girl's fair cheek, as she said in a low voice:

"Nothing is settled yet, nor even begun to be settled between Uncle Samson and myself, except …" She lifted her glorious gray eyes, and the brave courage of the young face was beautiful, but she did not go further and her companion could only guess at her wordless thought.

The streak of real Colorado weather had slipped across the prairies and in its cool refreshing the two young riders went slowly homeward.

Brown Stubble
'neath a Dome
of
Brass

VII

A house is built of brick and stone, with sills,
          and roof and piers,
But a home is built out of loving deeds that stand
          for a thousand years.

AUGUST ran into September, and September gave place to October. Engineers had figured the cost of squaring and leveling the ranches, and crucifying an old man's life-dream, and still no changes had been made. The woodland of "The Shadows" grew golden brown, the sumach and scrub oak on the slopes were a riot of purple and scarlet, every color of the rainbow shone in the frost-fired grasses along the winding road. The waters of the rock-bottom ford, deeper from the fall rains, splashed the varnish on the passing automobiles, the dreamy air of a Kansas October hung over the prairies; filling the hours with delight.

Yet all was not well in one corner of the great Kansas wheat belt. Edith Grannell who had been homeless for twelve years now had a home so pleasantly fastened about her that its ties were all the harder to break. Samson Grannell gave his niece no opportunity, nor excuse from his viewpoint, to consider the ending of her visit. Edith, however, went quietly forward with her own plans, although it was early September before she could make an opportunity to speak of them.

"I have a call to Chicago, Uncle Samson," she said one day when she opened her mail. "A schoolmate's mother writes that she wants me to fill a vacancy just made in a nurses' training school. It is the very thing I'd like to do. Of course, this is a little sudden, but I should be going soon anyhow."

"Why should you?" Grannell inquired in an even voice.

"Why? Because I can't stay here in idleness, now that I can earn my living. I don't want to offend you, Uncle Samson, by speaking of this, but I've taxed you long enough."

As she stood up before him, capable, determined, and winsomely attractive, she seemed fitted alike to adorn a home or to take care of herself, and Samson Grannell for the first time began to realize this.

"Would you stay if I needed you?" he asked without sign of offense in his voice.

"Oh, if you needed me, I would stay," Edith replied.

"Yes, I'm sure of it."

Grannell might as well have said, "Then you'll not go," so decisive was his tone.

And Edith did not go.

Captain Klews once told Jim Gledden that when Sam Grannell made up his mind to a thing there was nothing left to Providence but to get things ready for it. The very next day the housekeeper made a misstep on the cellar stairs, with the result of a hard fall, and a dislocated shoulder, and

Edith's training as a nurse began at once.

"I could hire someone, of course," her uncle said, "but I would rather have you, and since you are determined to go into wage earning, I'll pay you what I would a stranger."

"I couldn't let you do that," Edith insisted.

"Then I'll have to get someone who will, and let you go, although I need you and want you to stay here," Grannell replied.

That settled matters, and Samson Grannell had won the day. He had not yet confessed to himself that the ranchhouse would be strangely dreary without the presence of this sunny-spirited girl, and his conscience was as yet but dimly awake to what he had lost through twelve lost years.

A swift realization of how much life she had put into four walls now came to him. But it was as a selfish man sees, and Samson Grannell had still much to learn.

The Corner Stone

All was not well with Noel Waverly, who had never learned the swift fortune building art of a younger generation. So while those about him grew rich, he was finding it harder and harder to maintain himself.

In the day of the elder Helm he had given option jointly, in the event of his death, to the two ranches that had already acquired most of his once big holdings. Bad fortune had made it necessary later to mortgage the remainder to Isabel Helm, whom he chose in preference to Samson Grannell, with the understanding, of course, that Grannell should have the same option on a share if foreclosure should follow.

The mortgage was several months overdue, but Isabel Helm had not foreclosed.

"Damn a sentimental woman!" Grannell said often now. "Mrs. Helm is letting old Waverly drag behind with his interest when she could fix things. Homer's marriage will settle everything, and Homer will marry. This is an interesting game for the young folks, but they mustn't play it too long. How cocksure they are of themselves, never dreaming who makes most of the moves for them on this particular checker board. I'll have to settle some things with him about the Waverly land to make sure though, or that mother of his with her big brown eyes and cheeks growing red and white will get some sort of promise out of him. I've hung on till I'd die mad if this thing didn't go through."

The Corner Stone

Homer Helm went East early in October on business for his mother. Grannell reasoned that what was done in his absence might help to the quick culmination after his return.

One ranch, six thousand four hundred acres broad; every acre, save the building sites, in wheat — that was his dream for the future. Just as Noel Waverly with bowed white head dreamed of holding still to the woodland "Shadows," that his Mary had loved.

Homer Helm came to tell Edith good bye on the evening before he left home.

It was in the full of the hunter's moon, and a silver radiance made the night beautiful.

"I shall come home as soon as possible, for mother is not very well, and there are so many things to look after this fall. Meantime, I'll 'hope ever' for all good things for all good Kansans," he said as they stood at Edith's gateway. "This is a beautiful night to remember — one's blessings," he added, as he looked at

Edith's face in the moonlight.

Since that morning on Pawnee Rock they had not spoken of remembering. The old comradeship was lost for them, but a newer understanding existed unworded between them. The trivial purposes of each in the May time when they first went horseback riding together fell away before the stronger feeling of the autumn days.

"This is not like that other good-bye when you went away long ago, for I'll be back in twelve days instead of twelve years, yet I don't want to go. So many things might happen while I'm gone. I don't like good-byes, so I won't say any. I'll just run away now."

Homer gently lifted the girl's face between his hands and looked into her eyes, assured in mind that there was no shadow of truth in the gossip that had so misrepresented her. A moment later he was galloping away.

Edith Grannell stood long at the gate looking at the moonlight through tear-wet lashes.

"He is not a flirt," she said softly to herself. "He is not a selfish money-lover who wants only a rich girl for a wife. He's the grown-up little Homer Helm of long ago."

So many things did happen in Homer's absence, and afterward, that his anxious forecast was as a prophetic call.

Early in the next forenoon Samson Grannell sought out Noel Waverly. If the interview was harsh, it was perfectly plain and business-like, and no line of pity softened the face of the rich ranch owner, as he looked at the old plainsman, helpless before him.

"I read you like a book," he declared bluntly, unmindful that a little child with big pitying blue eyes sat behind her grandfather's chair, clutching the back of his elbow. "You've played the sob game to the end. You are going under now. If you'll just let Mrs. Helm settle with you, I'll give you a life lease, rent free, on five acres I own six miles west. You won't need it long. And you can put that child in an orphan asylum. You've kept her too long already."

It was not to taunt the old man with his brief life tenure, but the habitual thought of gain that made the younger, man consider how soon the five acres would revert to himself again. But strangely enough for the first time the word orphan asylum grated on his own ears.

"It's up on the ridge. There's no trees of course, but there's a good little two roomed house and a stable for a horse and cow. There's a spring, some way off, it's true, but you can save all the water you'll use in a rain-barrel, and what do you care for all this here at your time of life, Waverly? We are living in a day of real things, section lines and straight edges, not fanciful curves and imaginary sentimental ideas."

Noel Waverly knew all about that barren five-acre tract lost to a poor freeholder through debt; a dreary, sun-baked spot with unpainted dwelling, and weed-grown dooryard. For a few minutes he sat with bowed head. Then the spirit of the plainsman woke to life. The man who had hunted the buffalo and fought the Pawnee, who had herded cattle on the range, and held the land for coming occupation — the force without whom the great wheat belt had been impossible — this white-haired, keen-eyed man, standing erect with flashing eyes, hurled defiance at his enemy.

"I can read you like a book, Samson Grannell," he declared. "You let that niece of yours go homeless for years, till you wanted some means of controlling Homer Helm. Then you sent for her to make a match between them. Not for her sake, but your own. You'd turn her out tomorrow, same as you would me, if you didn't need her, for you want just one thing, money. You taunt me about my short life span. Why, man, I want to go and be with Mary Waverly again, if only I can save enough to protect my little Faith here and support her till she can take care of herself. She's never going to an orphan asylum. Poor as I am, I'm rich in one thing where you with your younger years and money are a pauper, and that's the riches of love. You can't know what that means. But Faith and I do.

"You talk about real things, as squares and straight lines. Did you ever see a section line? Most of the real things of life are the unseen things. And even the things you can see aren't straight lines. The rivers curve in and out I never saw a shower, blessing a burnt up Kansas prairie, falling from a square cloud; I never saw a three-cornered apple, nor an eight-sided stalk of wheat. And as to sentiment and imagination, out of sight of human eyes are dreams and hopes and loves and memories and home and heaven and God

Almighty who dwelleth not in temples made with men's hands, and who maketh the clouds His chariot.

"You can't understand life, Samson Grannell, until you learn what is real and what is false, until you get the angles out of your eyes, and the curves into your heart.

"And once for all," the old man now stood up erect and full of courage. "Once for all, remember, I come of a fighting generation, and I won't give up yet. The Arapahoes roped me and staked me out to die in the Cimarron country when I was nineteen, but I'm here yet. A wounded buffalo bull had me down but I killed him. The Comanches had their knives ready to get my scalp but Mary saved me. The Pawnees tied me to a stake to torture and burn me — but I was reserved for that five acre tract, seemingly! I'm never going to lay down while I can fight another lick. You hear what I say? Now, you leave my house and never darken that door again till you come in like a gentleman."

Grannell burst out in uncontrollable anger:

"It's not your house, you old pauper leach, and I'll never leave it till you agree —"

He got no further, for Noel Waverly's iron fist shot out straight before him with a force as fierce as it was swift, and unexpected, and Samson Grannell, the wheat king of his community, reeled backward and sprawled in an ignominious heap on the blue grass under the cottonwoods of the dooryard.

VIII

The mystery of the untried days
   I close my eyes from reading;
His will be done whose darkest ways
   To light and life are leading.
             — Whittier.

WON'T you come over here, and do something for me, please?" Little Faith Clover called across the ford to Edith Grannell who was loitering down by the creek on the afternoon after her uncle's visit to "The Shadows."

"How can I get across? The water is over the stepping stones," Edith answered.

"You can 'cat' across on the fence," Faith explained.

"To cat" meant to creep across on the water gate of the creek. Edith was lonely enough to do anything to pass off a part of the twelve days before her, so she "catted" quite gracefully considering the requirements of catting, and the narrowness of walking skirts.

"Will you come and see Dando?" Faith asked. "He wants you, I most know."

"If you both want me, I'll go, of course," Edith responded graciously.

So the two went together to the little home under the cottonwoods, where Noel Waverly was sitting with stern face, looking out at the peaceful prairies, beyond the valley, and the purple haze that folds down about them.

"I brought you something, Dando," Faith said softly, coming up behind him.

Noel Waverly was too much of a man to hold resentment against Edith on account of her name. He had wished all summer that he might meet her again, for he had not forgotten the little girl of long ago. But the Grannell household had little intercourse with the old man of "The Shadows."

"We know each other, Faith; he used to tell me stories when I was only a little bigger than you are. Can I do anything for you?" She turned to the old man, her face full of kindest interest.

Noel Waverly well knew that Samson Grannell would push matters to a finish now. In return for his fist would be Grannell's heel, or his own neck. The presence of Edith brought a new suggestion to him. He would lay the case before her. Delicately, and without offense, if possible, he would try to secure her help. He must do something. This was a drowning man's effort.

"Won't you sit down awhile and let me talk to you, Miss Grannell? Forgive an old man for troubling you. It may be you can do me a favor." There was something of the chivalry of the olden days about Noel Waverly. He must have been a man of attractive presence in his younger years.

"I should be glad to do anything for you that I could do," Edith assured him.

"You know the history of these two ranches on either side of me, and how the owners sit waiting for me to die — forgive me for saying it — to square their boundaries."

"Yes, I know," Edith answered. "And I've always felt sorry for you."

There was no doubting her sincerity nor her genuine sympathy, and both were a balm to the old man's sore heart.

"I'm not a money-maker. I lived too long in the days when ten thousand dollars was a fortune. My sons died young. Then I began to sell off my land, and at last my son-in-law, Jim Clover, came to grief. Sickness, poor crops, cattle perishing in the blizzard, endorsing notes at the bank for friends, all combined against him. Jim was honest to the penny, but misfortune followed him. His wife, my daughter, died the day Faith was born. The next year my wife died. Jim lost his life in a blizzard that winter. I took up the burden he laid down and paid every cent that nobody should lose anything through me or mine. And I took my little grandchild to my heart and gave her a home. But now just as soon as Homer Helm comes into his property, he can foreclose, and drive me out, me and the little girl I've been father and mother to."

"Mr. Helm wouldn't turn you out." Edith's face was full of surprise and sorrow.

"Oh, yes, he will. You don't know how ravenous land can make a man for more land. As long as Mrs. Helm holds the property she will befriend me. But she may have to give up the control at any time, or, she might die. Then I'm at Homer's mercy. I thought maybe you wouldn't mind saying a word of what you think about it to him sometime." Waverly's voice faltered.

Stories of Homer Helm's increasing love of property that she had denied to herself came to Edith now with a new meaning. Yet how could he who seemed so manly and gentle, he who needed for nothing, turn an old man out of his home?

"I should hate him and distrust him always, if he did that," she said to herself. Aloud she said, "I can't believe Homer — Mr. Helm — would foreclose on you. But I'll speak to him anyhow. He has never talked about his business affairs to me. Why don't you go to Mrs. Helm and ask her to intercede for you with her son? If I can do anything for you, I will be glad. I must go now," and she rose to leave him.

"I thank you so much, Miss Grannell. It was such a little while ago that you and Homer were children here. Little sweethearts then. I remember how lonely he was when you went away. Seemed like he'd never get over missing you. He was never quite the same boy after that."

The old man's face beamed with gratitude as his visitor shook his hand and went her way.

The next evening Noel Waverly with little Faith went to see Isabel Helm. There was a flush on her cheeks, and her eyes were glowing with a strange but kindly light as she listened to his plea. Doing good to others had marked the way of her life.

"I'll never foreclose on you, Noel. Homer has not mentioned marrying to me yet. I have always felt that my husband's will has been an embarrassment to him. I'll tell you what I'll do. Life is uncertain — and so are marriages —"she added with a smile. "I'll send for a notary tomorrow morning, and have a signed statement of my wishes, duly witnessed, for you."

Her cheeks were deeply pink and her eyes were shining as she bade the old man good-night.

The next morning the notary's services were not needed. The red flush, token of irregular heart action, had warned in vain. Isabel Helm had slipped out of life smilingly, as one who falls asleep, and Homer Helm entered unhampered into his own.

Noel Waverly's fist had helped tremendously to bring a speedy ending to this land business for Samson Grannell. He was determined now to thresh the matter out with Isabel Helm, who was unjustly keeping him out of his share of the Waverly holdings. The young folks he could whip into shape afterward. As he was riding home from a two days' business trip he stopped at the top of the slope by "The Shadows." He was so absorbed in his own calculations that he did not notice the presence of Faith Clover until she stood beside the car looking up at him.

"Are you waiting for Dando?" she asked timidly. "He's gone over to Helm's to the big red barn over there. Mrs. Helm went to heaven yesterday morning, and—"

"What did you say? That Mrs. Helm is dead?" Grannell asked, clutching the side of the car.

"Yes, I did," Faith answered simply.

"What are you doing here?" Grannell did not know why he asked the question. His mind was dazed by the news he had heard.

"Oh, I am playing like the prince will come home pretty soon or the princess will cry."

"And what do you know about the prince?" Grannell asked, while looking shrewdly at the innocent face before him.

"I play like he loves the princess and they will marry and live happily ever after."

"The kid comes honestly by her notions, she is just like the old man. But Homer owns everything now!' Grannell thought as he tried not to exult.

"Well, what do you know about the princess," he asked.

"She won't love the prince if he takes Dando's trees and house, and everything. She told Dando she knew the prince wouldn't never do that"

Grannell did not care to hear any more. Now was his time to act. The extermination of Waverly and the small gain to be acquired possessed him. Narrow purposes are no less dominant than broad, generous ones. Either may become the master of a soul.

That evening came the crisis as the two sat together in the twilight after tea talking of this sudden death of their neighbor.

"Everything belongs to Homer now, of course," Grannell declared. "He will make no concessions to Waverly. He has wanted to be rid of the old man too long."

"Are you sure of that?" Edith asked, glad that the evening shadows hid her face.

"I know it absolutely. Have known it ever since Homer came home from college. Why do you ask?"

"Because I would despise a man forever who would turn a poor old man out of his home just to add a few more acres to his own big farm," Edith replied.

"Would you?" The voice cut like a steel blade. "I'm glad it's not in my power to do it. You would despise me."

Six months ago her words could not have hurt him. Their unconscious stab tonight was index of how much she had come into his life.

"Oh, Uncle Samson, you know I couldn't do that" Edith could say nothing more.

"And you'll take back what you say about despising the man who makes old Waverly come to time?" He followed up the advantage gained.

"Never!" Edith spoke decisively.

Samson Grannell shifted his plans at once.

"Homer will marry some rich girl, or one with prospects," he said after a long pause, "or at least one with good business sense about property values," he added casually. "He'd be sure to cut any girl who interfered or objected to his squaring his ranch and making it more productive. He's set on that. All any girl he cares for would need to do would be to agree with him. I know what I'm saying, Edith."

"Little white lies must be all right if they serve a big purpose," Grannell reasoned to himself. "This affair between the young folks must go no further until things are made safe. Edith is a sensible girl, and if it comes down to brass tacks, she's too smart to let anything stand in her way. Folks in love, too, will give up anything. I was a fool that way myself once, ready to give up every principle I ever had for a girl."

So Grannell philosophised. But the trouble with the philosopher is that he may mistake selfishness for wisdom.

"Edith, you've been kept here too closely nursing the cripple. How would you like to run down to Kansas City and do some shopping? Every woman likes to shop, and you could go this week." Grannell shifted easily from one line to another.

"I would like it very much," Edith said faintly.

The world had gone out from under her feet tonight. Her uncle had always known Homer Helm. He must know what many others had hinted to her before, the young man's love of riches — and she was penniless. The game she had played in the early summer had become a bitter reality now, and she must play on to the end.

The Corner Stone

Homer Helm had no opportunity of meeting Edith before his mother's funeral. Two evenings after the burial, he came to call at the Grannell home.

"Edith has gone to Kansas City to do some shopping," Grannell explained smoothly. "She left early this morning. You know when a woman has clothes on the brain, you can't stop 'em, and this is bargain week down there. Edith's got good business sense. Of course, she has reason to expect that I'll do well by her sometime — she's the only heir I have in the world — if she doesn't oppose my wishes, and she won't do that. By the way, she thinks just as I do about old Waverly. She'd have him out tomorrow, if she had her way."

By his own standards, Samson Grannell felt that he was putting on his niece the value the rich young ranchman must highly approve. Moreover, he trusted to the willingness of a young lover to do whatever the girl he loved should desire. He had been the same kind of a fool once himself. But be had worshiped too long at one shrine now to see what lay back of the set face and dark eyes before him. His idol never crumbled. How could he understand the sorrow and disappointment of the younger man?

He would keep the two apart till his point was gained. That would soon be done. Then matters would shape up all right and they would thank him in the end.

The Corner Stone

By his adroit planning no opportunity came to the two young people to question each other or come to an understanding. Edith waited in sadness for a settlement of the Waverly matter, while Homer set himself sternly to the task of ignoring and forgetting a girl whose motives were so unworthy.

The golden light of October lay on all the prairies. The purple haze of autumn curtained the horizon. - But the light was a glare and the purple a deepening shadow to two young hearts who had found dross where they had hoped to find gold.

The days came and went, but Blackstone and White Rock cantered no more together along the level roads. Homer did not call at the Grannell ranch except on such business as might be transacted out of doors, with the owner of the ranch.

Edith gave no opportunity for any interview when they met by chance in the same company. Gossip took a new tack and busied itself — but neither one heeded a word for nor against the other. The Helm house was listed in the rural free delivery route and old Captain Mews had few occasions to report to Homer what Jim Gledden gathered up by the way.

In spite of Grannell's protest the creek was bridged in November. But largely on account of his protest the structure was a cheap affair, pending the time when a permanent one should be built on the new straight road to the north.

Silver Snows and Scarlet Sunsets

IX

A little child shall lead them.
— Isaiah.

TWO months passed after the death of Isabel Helm, and Christmas was approaching. Homer Helm had not yet pressed the foreclosure of the mortgage he held against "The Shadows," but Noel Waverly knew a reckoning day was near, and he had not even enough money to cover the over-due interest. He knew, too, that there was small chance for Santa Claus to remember little Faith this year. Few heartaches are like that of knowing that a trusting child must be disappointed on Christmas morning.

December had been unusually mild, and the day before Christmas was almost balmy in its warmth, with heavy brown shadows in the northwest, token of an approaching storm.

"I saw old Noel Waverly starting to town a while ago," Samson Grannell said to Edith at lunch time. "Some men who can't pay their debts have plenty to spend at Christmas, it seems."

"It might mean a great deal to little Faith," Edith ventured.

"The sooner she gets over expecting such things the better. Besides, there's a change coming. This weather is unnatural, and there's a storm mixing in the northwest right now. The old man's a fool to start on such a long ride with that slow old pony. I'm going to town myself in the car pretty soon." Christmas bad a new meaning to him now, with Edith in his borne, but it was a selfish man's Christmas withal. "If those packages that I ordered aren't in yet, I'll wait in town till the morning train. But if they are, I can make it there and back before dark. Noel will be till in the night getting home," he added, "and the young one will be there by herself. It's a mercy if she doesn't up set the lamp, or something. She ought to be in an orphan asylum as I've always said."

It would have been easy for Grannell to have taken his old neighbor in his car for the trip to town. But Noel had ordered him not to darken the Waverly door till he could come in like a gentleman. That had hurt worse than the old fist that sent him headlong to the ground in a most ungentlemanly manner. He'd show the old fighting brute how a gentleman can get to town and home again in comfort. He passed the pony and its rider on the way, both going and coming, but if be distinguished them from the dust of the earth, he made no sign. The wind was rising before he left town, and a great drop in the temperature foretold the uncoiling of a blizzard from that frowning dust brown northwest that would soon be whirling across the prairies in a fury of snow and bitter ravening cold. But the storm came more swiftly than Grannell had anticipated, so be made his car snug from the north blast, and sped onward in the gathering darkness. Far behind him Noel Waverly, hugging the little treasure that should brighten his loved one's Christmas morn, with the thinner blood of old age, bent bravely against the wind as he urged his faithful "Kit Carson" onward in the teeth of the black terror sweeping down on him.

Night fell quickly. A swirl of sleet made the road treacherous. Grannell had to slacken his speed and feel his way slowly and carefully, while, like the hare and the tortoise, the old pony and rider gained on the big machine. It skidded perilously as its driver went crashing down the winding trail toward the new bridge. It was not well built, as Grannell knew, and he knew, too, who had most influenced the commissioners in cheapening that building. But he cursed it and its builders as he remembered that the approach on one side was already caving away. He knew what might happen to him if he hit that side at an angle. But the sleet put out the eyes of the automobile and he plunged on blindly in the darkness.

Meanwhile, at home, Edith watched the night and the storm come down together. She had no anxiety for her uncle. He must be waiting in town overnight. Christmas time meant slow trains and choked express cars. But her heart grew heavy as she remembered little Faith.

"I can't bear to think of it," she cried at last, wrapping herself against the cold. "She might try to go out to meet her grandfather and get lost herself. I know every foot of the path," and the pang of haunting memories of summer strolls along that woodland way came sharp to her heart.

Every foot of the road was a battle in spite of her knowing. Beyond the bridge something seemed to catch at her ankle. It must have been only a crooked stick, but it felt to her gloved hand like the brass rim of a wind shield, At last she found herself in the room where little Faith sat in the dark and cold.

Edith brought in wood and soon a blazing fire filled the room with its warmth and cheer.

"It was so black and lonesome without Dando," Faith said, as she snuggled down close to Edith's side. "I'm so glad you are here. Will you stay till he comes?"

Yes, I'll stay till he comes," Edith said with sinking doubt in her heart, as she thought of the old man out in the storm.

"Did you know you are my playlike princess?" Faith asked, putting both arms lovingly about the girl's neck.

"Am I? I'm glad" Edith replied.

"And Homer is the prince and I want so much to know if the story's ended. Your runcle broke my castle, and I couldn't see you anymore and I don't know if it ended."

Edith could not understand, so she only hugged the little curly head to her shoulder. And sitting thus they made a pretty picture in the firelight.

"There's Dando now," Faith cried as the kitchen door opened; but it was Homer Helm who stood before them.

Faith gave him a shy greeting, half conscious of the chill that had come in with him.

"Do you want to see Dando? He's gone to town and it's so cold, she came to stay with me till he comes back, isn't she good?"

Homer looked in surprise at Edith. Had she come out in this storm to bring comfort to a little girl whose grandfather she would see made houseless tomorrow? While Edith wondered what could bring Homer Helm on Christmas eve of all eves of the year to the home of the man whom he meant to drive out of doors. But a wall had come between them. Since his mother's death, when they met the hard look in his eyes was confronted with the scorn in hers. His face was stern now as if he meant to carry out a purpose in spite of her presence. But his eyes were gentle when he turned to Faith. The heart of a child is quick to read character, and Faith saw only a friend.

"Will your Dando hang up his stocking tonight?" Homer asked.

"I've got it hanged for him, 'cause he might forget," Faith replied. "Once he did forget and Santa never left him anything."

"Well, I've just come from Santa Claus," Homer went on. "He couldn't get over here tonight. One of his reindeer threw a shoe, so I'll take care of Dando's stocking for him right now, and then I must be going."

"What a funny thing for Dando. Tell me what it is, and, cross my heart, I won't tell."

Faith fingered at a long envelope crowded into the old man's woollen hose.

"Just a paper, part printed, part written, with some red lines and a gold seal — I call it a sunflower." Homer replied with a strangely defiant ring in his tone.

Faith looked up at the young man. The eyes of a child see far.

"Does it say Dando must pay intrist?" she asked earnestly.

"It says he needn't ever pay intrist, any more. It's the mortgage my mother held overdue for nearly a year. It's Dando's Christmas present. I shall not die poorer because for a few years I let an old man live in security and peace. If I do, prosperity isn't worth the price."

Homer was not looking at Faith, nor speaking to her. He was looking straight at Edith Grannell.

"Oh, you are a prince, a prince, a prince," Faith danced about in joy. "It will make Dando so glad, glad, glad. I wish he'd come." A shadow flitted across the sunny face, as the storm rattled at the windows.

"Won't you sit down, and wait for Dando. And please, please tell me is the story ended?" Faith pulled Homer into a chair beside Edith, and stood up before the two with eager questioning eyes.

"Is the story ended?" she repeated.

"You tell us what the story is. We don't know anything about it," Edith said, trying hard to control her voice.

"Why, it's. just your ownselves' story, and I didn't make it up, I just played like, only I never did know if it ended and you lived happily ever after. I'll tell you how I played it for you."

The young people involuntarily drew closer together, and there swept over them both a sense of the nearness of innocence and love and trust to the real heart of life.

"I lived in my castle bushes most all summer," Faith began, "but it's broke now. And when you first came princing out of fairy land from your castle where the big red barn is, I just play like you know, and she came with wild flowers up from the creek, that's my Missouri river, and s'prized you, I played like you were a real prince and princess, and would love each other. You came so often. I tried not to miss you, for it was such a sweet story."

Faith looked fondly at each young face before her, as she prattled on.

"The prince found your little pin and kept it, not 'cause he's a stealer, sure he isn't no stealer. He just wanted it 'cause you are his princess, I played like. But you went to Pawnee Rock and my castle got broke down, and White Face got in and tore up the vines and I never did know if you lived happily ever after, but you must, 'cause you are so good to Dando — and bringed that nice Christmas gift for Santa Claus, and the princess said you wouldn't never turn us out, she knew you wouldn't, she told Dando so one day, and she asked him to go see your mamma, 'cause she knew your mamma would take care of Dando's home and trees and creek. But your mamma went to heaven too soon." Faith's sunny face clouded now.

Homer tried once to look into Edith's face, but her eyes were for the little child only.

"Is that all of your story?" she asked in a low voice.

"You went to Pawnee Rock and Dando says, and he knows, that folks that love on Pawnee Rock love always and always. Please tell me is the story ended?" Faith asked.

Edith made no reply, so Faith turned to Homer who had risen to his feet.

"Not yet," he answered, "I'm not a stealer, Faith, and I 'hope ever.'"

X

Oh, Earth! thou hast not any wind that blows
    Which is not music; every weed of thine
    Pressed rightly, glows with aromatic wine;
And every humble hedgerow flower that grows,
    And every little brown bird that doth sing,
Hath something greater than itself, and bears
    A living word to every living thing.
              — Richard Realf.

MEANWHILE Noel Waverly fought his way over the long miles against the blizzard's rage, trusting to Kit Carson's wild instinct to carry him safely through.

"They can keep their old gasoline gigs," he said to himself, "and I'll keep my old half-breed Indian pony. The sleet hasn't blinded his glass eyes, he don't need skid chains, and he's got some mind about what I want; while a car like Grannell's would go straight to hell, left to itself, and not care how many goggle-eyed, big-gloved chauffeurs it took along."

As he reached the top of the slope near his home, an agonizing wail came to his ears. Again it came, then the storm swallowed it.

"Somebody lost or hurt. I'm pretty cold, too. But we must find 'em, Kit. Go on," he urged.

The pony plunged down toward the caving approach to the new bridge over 'the creek. And Noel Waverly, because he had been bred to danger, knew how to find and meet it. The old frame had still the vigor of the plains-hardened muscles, and the old arms a strength many a softer sinewed young man might envy. He forgot the cold, and the darkness, and the seventy-five years that had sapped his vitality.

Down under the big touring car, Samson Grannell lay like a dying man, it seemed to Noel Waverly, and Noel knew the marks of that great Enemy. Then came the miracle — old as the miracles down in Capernaum — the strength of soul that nerves the arm because the loving heart will not pass suffering humanity by Noel Waverly, old, cold, and alone, wrestled with the big inert weight that was crushing the life out of his enemy, and would not yield, until at last he won. With a marvelous grip he lifted the crushed and broken body of the helpless man to the back of his slow old pony, and, fighting his way on foot through the darkness and bitter cold, he led Kit with his half-dying burden up to the big, un-mortgaged Grannell house. The self-taught surgeon of a younger day knew well the many ways of saving life, of slipping back wrenched joints, and stanching the flow of bleeding arteries. The first, and only, aid to the injured served as well in the rich man's home on this storm-wracked night of the twentieth century, as it had done in the day of arrow and tomahawk on the far desolate plains of an unwon wilderness.

"How did you happen to find me? How could you ever get me from under that heavy machine? How could you get me on your pony and up here through the drifts? How could you fix these injuries alone?" Samson Grannell asked the questions feebly one after another as he lay at length, awaiting the coming of dawn.

"And, why didn't you leave me to die?" he added, with a groan, "a man that's been a brute to you all these years?"

"Don't ask too many questions right now. You better keep that shoulder still, and bear the pain like a man. The doctor will fix you up easier as soon as he can get at you. This is just my old-fashioned way of surgery. I belong to a generation that's about gone out."

The unconscious stab of the words hurt worse than any wound on Samson Grannell's bruised body. Like a vision came the grip on life, real life, that may belong to a man poor in purse, old in years, but young and rich, abundantly and eternally prosperous, in human love.

"Waverly," he queried feebly, "I always thought that you were a hard-fisted plainsman in your younger years, and you've had enough bad luck to make you hate the world. What has brought you to a tender-hearted old age?"

"The corner stone of life is love," Noel Waverly replied, as he sat beside the bed, gently stroking Samson Grannell's wrenched right arm, "and it may be the love of a little child. With all their dreams and odd gentle ways, sometimes they can see right through what's only a solid wall to us. Faith Clover made me a lover, not a hater of men. If I had my way there'd be no orphan asylums, but a home for every child. You shut out the biggest joy of your life, Samson Grannell, when you sent your little niece away from you. But you are a young man yet. When you get well, you'll measure life in curves as well as straight lines. And you'll see that the unseen things, the feelings and hopes and longings of the human soul are bigger than the things we measure by the yardstick and weigh on scales, and value in dollars and cents."

The sun of a December day had slipped down the west, and hung a moment to send one last broad sweep of radiance far up the crystal skies — a good-night to the world as glorious as the grand good-morning of an August day.

On the top of Pawnee Rock, Homer Helm and Edith Grannell stood looking to the west, where the after-glow of a winter sunset burned in an ineffable grandeur.

"Edith, do you remember when we were here last August that I told you I had never forgotten anything of the days of our childhood, and so I hadn't forgotten the day when you went away and left a little boy so lonely?" Homer turned to his companion with the question.

"I remember," Edith answered, still looking out toward the radiant splendor of the winter sky.

"He looked up to you then. He's been looking up, to you ever since. He was a lonely shy little boy who lived over the days of childhood until the best things they held became enshrined as the best things of his manhood. The memory of a good-bye kiss staid with that little boy who was two years older and not nearly so big as the little girl then — staid, until he became a man ever so much bigger and stronger than the grown-up little girl. And he knows, for Faith Clover told him, that she is gentle, and kind to the poor, and that it is not money but manliness that counts with her. Edith, I've wished so long for an hour like this, but I could not be sure that you would wish for it, too. You forgot all about me years ago and I'm not worthy of a place in your memory."

"I've been told over and over that the little boy grew up to care for rich girls only, or girls with 'prospects,' but I never forgot that day," Edith said softly.

And then, somehow, two strong arms were about her and on her lips love left its first sweet kiss.

"Forgive me, Edith, it was only the little boy who was glad again — there's no use trying that" Homer broke off and stood silent beside her.

"Edith, I did find your monogram pin, as Faith said, and I meant to give it to you the next day. I was only teasing. But I lost it myself, and now those markings I cut here last August are gone, too."

Homer looked down on the rock at his feet whereon he had cut the lines,

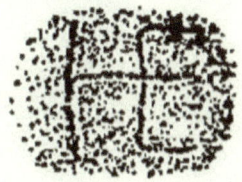

"The symbol that I put here has faded. Does that which it symbolizes endure? Edith, may I hope ever? May not this monogram really mean Homer, Edith, one forever henceforth?"

He had taken Edith's hands in his and she let them rest there.

"Faith Clover says, 'Whoever loves on Pawnee Rock will love always and always,'" she murmured softly.

"'And live happily ever after,'" Homer added, "because the corner stone of life is love."

Edith looked up. The manly form, the strong face, the dark eyes filled with all the longing of the years treasured since the parting moment of a far away day of boy hood; underneath her feet was the solid old Pawnee Rock; out yonder the splendor of scarlet and silver, the radiant twilight afterglow at the end of a perfect day!

The Corner Stone: Historical Context

About the Author

Margaret Hill McCarter describes her protagonist, Edith Grannell, from the perspective of Edith's uncle Samson Grannell: "As she stood up before him, capable, determined, and winsomely attractive, she seemed fitted alike to adorn a home or to take care of herself." This was likely a bold position to take when the story was published in 1915 - that a woman might be equally suited to be a wife - or not. But it was not so surprising to be taken by McCarter. In addition to being a wife and homemaker, Margaret Hill McCarter was a successful author of stories, books and poetry. (Center for Kansas Studies; Kansas Historical Society 2011)

Born in Indiana, Margaret Hill McCarter came to Topeka in 1888 at about the age of 28 to teach English. Two years later, she married Dr. William McCarter. She was active in the community and in politics. A member of the Republican National Women's Committee, she was the first woman to address a national convention of a major political party. McCarter was introduced at the 1920 Republican National Convention as "well known as a writer and a staunch Republican by inheritance as well as by belief." Outside the Convention, six members of the National Woman's Party protested, holding a banner reading "No self-respecting woman should wish or work for the success of a party that ignores her sex," the 1872 quote from Susan B. Anthony. While McCarter and the National Woman's Party protesters had different, even opposing, approaches, both sides helped to advance the cause of women securing the right to vote. By directly participating in the political process and by protesting to raise awareness McCarter and the National Woman's Party protestors helped women to become more fully engaged in the political domain that governed their lives. Two months after the Republican National Convention, the Nineteenth Amendment to the Constitution was ratified giving women the right to vote. (National Photo Company; Hart 1920)

About the Artist

James Allen St. John was born in Chicago October 1, 1872, the son of artists Josephus Allen St. John and Susan Hely St. John. He was hired by A. C. McClurg & Co. in 1915 to illustrate the second work in the Tarzan series by Edgar Rice Burroughs. In addition to the illustrations for the series of books by Burroughs, St. John provided illustrations for other authors publishing with McClurg, including Margaret Hill McCarter. An artist and illustrator, St. John painted portraits, created art for magazine covers, and designed war posters promoting, for example, Liberty Bonds and the Salvation Army. St. John authored one work which he also illustrated, *The Face in the Pool*. (Estes; Vadeboncoeur 2011)

The Corner Stone

About the Setting

Ms. McCarter had written dozens of stories and several books prior to publishing *The Corner Stone*. Her storytelling reflected contemporary life in Kansas, which she conveyed with fondness. *The Corner Stone* was set in the area around Pawnee Rock, in central Kansas (see map below), near the Arkansas River and the Atchison-Topeka-Santa Fe Railroad.

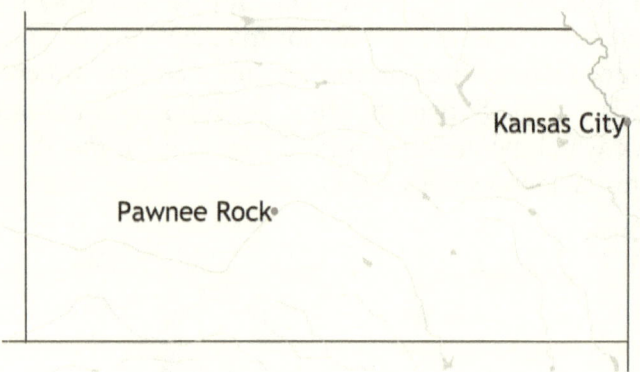

In addition to having a place of importance in her story, Pawnee Rock had a place of importance in her life. McCarter tells the story of the history of Pawnee Rock within *The Corner Stone:*

"Tell me about this rock, while we are resting," Edith said as they sat down facing the great silent land to the south.

The Corner Stone

"It used to be ever so much higher. It's been chipped and chopped off for commercial purposes. You know the grip of commercial purposes." Homer checked his tongue, as he remembered Samson Grannell. "It was a landmark on the old Santa Fe Trail, a citadel of the Plains in Noel Waverly's day, a monument to more tragedies than any other one spot in North America. This was the corner stone on which the civilization of the West was builded, a thing to rest on and to fight from.

In response to damage to the site from the mining mentioned in *The Corner Stone*, the Women's Kansas Day Club of which McCarter was a member, acquired Pawnee Rock in 1908. The club dedicated a monument at the site on May 14, 1912. Given her personal commitment to preserving the site, it is understandable that she would feature Pawnee Rock prominently in her storytelling.

"There were more Indian fights right here — it got its name from an awful Pawnee battle; more rescuers and refugees have stood on this cliff, the pursuers, and the pursued; more nameless graves and unburied dead in the soil below us. Sometimes it was the white man, and sometimes the red man, who held the fortress. The Indians could see from the top here to old Fort Zarah on the east and Fort Larned on the west. They could count the size of the wagon trains starting out from either place, and when they got to the foot of this bluff somebody perished, for this was the place of sepulchre."

The Corner Stone

This detailed section from "Map Showing the Atchison, Topeka & Santa Fe Railroad and its Auxiliary Roads in the State of Kansas," ((G. W. and C. B. Colton & Co. 1886), see below) shows Pawnee Rock situated directly on the Santa Fe rail line, not far from the Arkansas River flowing south of the railroad. Fort Zarah is about 16 miles to the northeast of Pawnee Rock, and Fort Larned about 8 miles to the southwest. While the small section of the map reproduced here offers geographic context for *The Corner Stone*, the original larger map, viewable online, represents a treasure trove of history across the state, including drainage, rivers, lakes, railroads, and the big population centers – Topeka, Leavenworth, and Kansas City, along with countless small settlements.

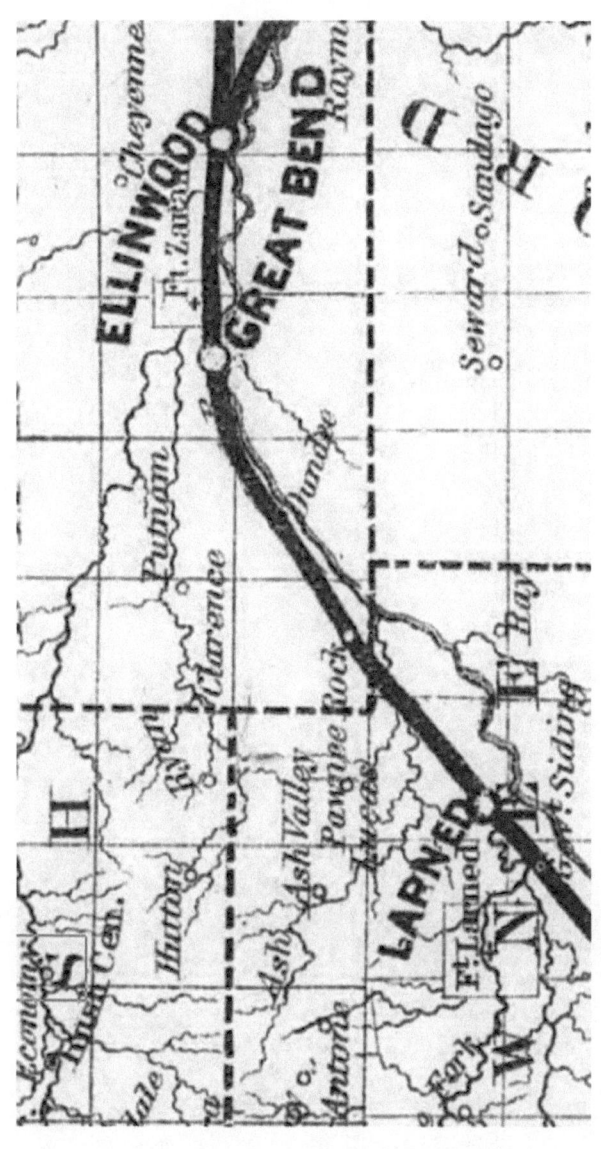

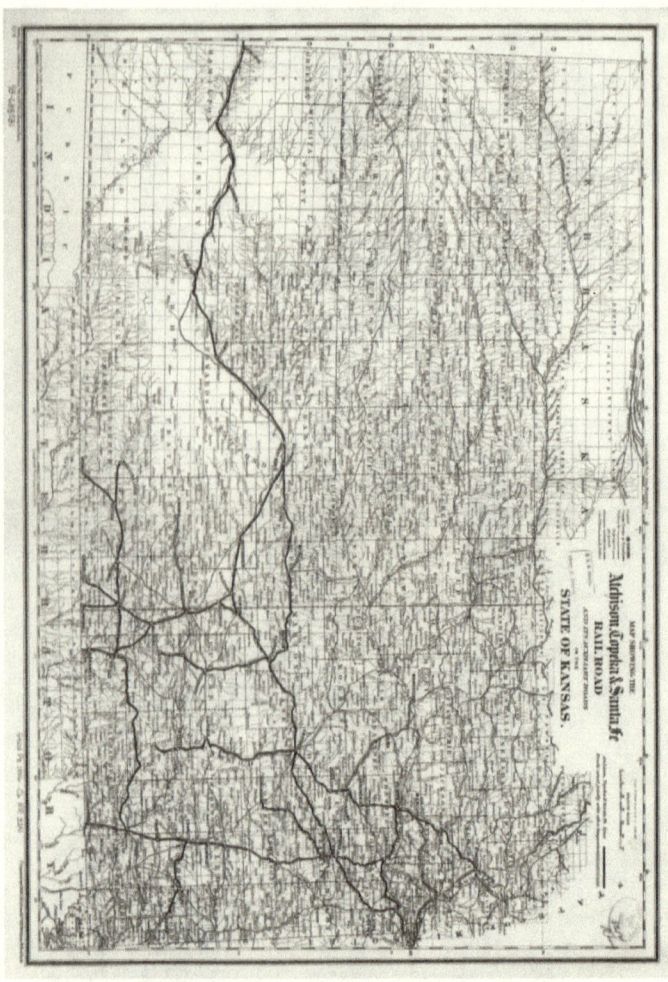

A timeline of events in Kansas history and events within the story provides additional context for the setting, and greater appreciation for the relationship between the author and her story. McCarter was born in May 1860, shortly before the Homestead Act came into effect, and only a few months before the State of Kansas was admitted to the Union. The Indian Removal Act of 1830 and the Homestead Act of 1862 were responsible for essentially forced emigration of Indian tribes into and then out of the region. Of the settlers who arrived, there were sharp divides between those who supported slavery and those who did not, resulting in violence over the issue that came to be referred to as "Bleeding Kansas" in the years just prior to McCarter's birth. Ultimately, Kansas was admitted to the United States as a slave-free state, just as the country became embroiled in the Civil War, from 1861 to 1865.

McCarter referred to events relating to these circumstances in her books and stories, including the hostilities between Indians and settlers, the back-breaking work of homesteading, and consequences of the Civil War. For example, McCarter introduces one of her characters, "Captain Klews," early in The Corner Stone, as "the one-armed postmaster." The reader doesn't learn until midway through the story that the arm was lost in war, when McCarter writes, "If ever Klews longed for the lost arm left on the battle field, he longed for it now that he might shake two fists every time he heard the name of Grannell." If Klews was an old man at the time McCarter tells the story (see timeline, below), it seems most likely her character lost his arm in the American Civil War. McCarter provided additional historical depth in the story told by the old plainsman, Noel Waverly, to his granddaughter, Faith. In the story, we learn that Waverly was a young scout, riding on the prairie, caught off guard by a group of Comanche Indians. Riding for his life, Waverly made his way to Pawnee Rock when his horse stumbled and broke its leg. The young scout was saved from the Indians' arrows by the riflery of a young woman on Pawnee Rock. That woman, Mary, had been stationed there to watch over settlers waiting for a wagon train from the fort. Mary became the love of Waverly's life and eventually, Faith's grandmother. Estimating Waverly's age in the story with respect the events of the day (see timeline, below), this vignette provides perspective on the exchanges of violence that were occurring as Indians were being moved into and out of the region, and settlers were taking over increasingly greater amounts of what had been recognized Indian territory. These incidents occurred in a timeframe largely before McCarter was born, but certainly accessible within the memory of her family and community.

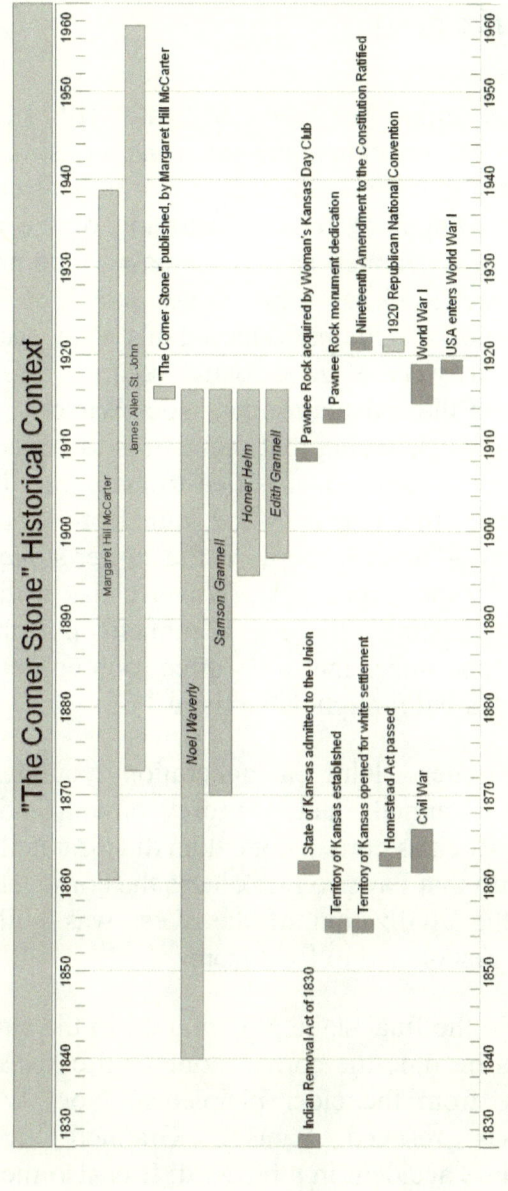

"The Corner Stone" Historical Context

The Corner Stone

About the Story

In telling her story, Margaret Hill McCarter evolves the understanding of what constitutes the corner stone of life as the theme that runs throughout. The story begins with an illustration of the disdain that Samson Grannell has for the past, when he refers to Pawnee Rock as "the corner stone of all the tragedies of the Plains," sharing his view that "Our best security is a good bank security." Grannell disparages the old plainsman, Noel Waverly, whose land he covets, saying that the man is too attached to his home: "When a man is tied to his home like that he knocks the corner stone out from under his prosperity — and prosperity is the corner stone of life with us." Not surprisingly, Waverly has a different view, suggesting "if he'd [Grannell] put the real corner stone under that little three roomed house she [Grannell's wife] might have lived."

Homer Helm, a generation younger than Samson Grannell, had a more romantic view of Pawnee Rock as corner stone than did Grannell. Helm tells Edith that Pawnee Rock "was the corner stone on which the civilization of the West was builded, a thing to rest on and to fight from."

In the final stage of evolution in the story arc, love has become the corner stone of life. This is the message from the elder plainsman, Noel Waverly, who has rescued Samson Grannell from an automobile accident in a blizzard. It is also the end to the story-in-a-story, when standing atop Pawnee Rock, Homer tells Edith that the "corner stone of life is love."

About the Publication

This story has been rendered painstakingly from an original copy of the work. With minor exceptions, nothing was intentionally added or omitted from the original work. The committed exceptions include two cases in which Samson Grannell's name was printed originally as "Grannel". Exceptions of omission are most likely quotations that were not rendered properly.

Historical Context References

Center for Kansas Studies. "Margaret Hill McCarter." Map of Kansas Literature.

http://www.washburn.edu/reference/cks/mapping/mccarter.

Estes, A. B. "J. Allen St. John, Information on the artist's early life and career." ERBzine.

http://www.erbzine.com/mag6/0602.html.

G. W. and C. B. Colton & Co. (1886). Map Showing the Atchison, Topeka & Santa Fe Railroad and its Auxiliary Roads in the State of Kansas. New York, Rufus Adams: Atchison, Topeka and Santa Fe Railroad in the state of Kansas. Shows drainage, cities and towns, township and county boundaries, and the railroad network with emphasis on the main line.

http://hdl.loc.gov/loc.gmd/g4201p.rr003240

Hart, G. L. (1920). Official Report of the Proceedings of the Seventeenth Republican National Convention. New York, New York.

http://archive.org/stream/officialreportof00repuiala#page/n101/mode/2up.

Kansas Historical Society (2011). "Margaret Hill McCarter." Kansapedia: People.

http://www.kshs.org/kansapedia/margaret-hill-mccarter/12143.

National Photo Company Women of Protest: Photographs from the Records of the National Woman's Party. Washington, D.C., Library of Congress.

http://hdl.loc.gov/loc.mss/mnwp.160074.

Vadeboncoeur, J. J. (2011, 2011). "J. Allen St. John." Illustrators.

http://www.bpib.com/illustrat/stjohn.htm.

www.ingramcontent.com/pod-product-compliance
Lightning Source LLC
Chambersburg PA
CBHW020250150626
46552CB00020B/741